Going Postal

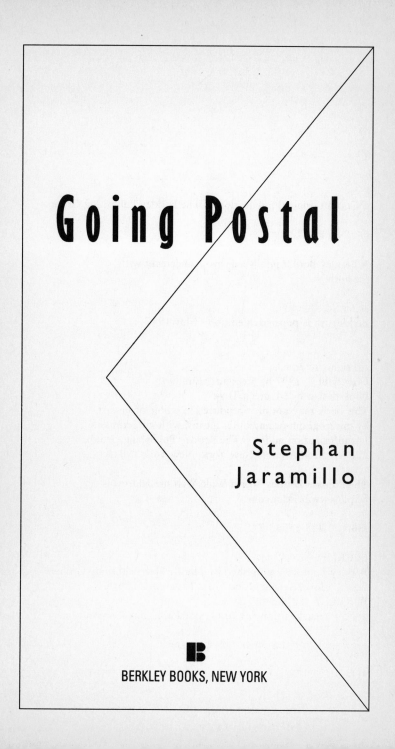

Going Postal

Stephan
Jaramillo

BERKLEY BOOKS, NEW YORK

This is an original publication of The Berkley Publishing Group.

GOING POSTAL

A Berkley Book / published by arrangement with
the author

PRINTING HISTORY
Berkley trade paperback edition / May 1997

The Putnam Berkley World Wide Web site address is
http://www.berkley.com

ISBN: 0-425-15768-7

BERKLEY®
Berkley Books are published by The Berkley Publishing Group,
200 Madison Avenue, New York, New York 10016.
BERKLEY and the "B" design
are trademarks belonging to Berkley Publishing Corporation.

PRINTED IN THE UNITED STATES OF AMERICA

10   9   8   7   6   5   4   3

Going Postal

Caveat

The following is a true story. Some of the names have been changed to disguise people I still have to deal with. Other shit has been changed to nail the fuckers I hate.

However, my family should strongly keep in mind that this is a work of !!FICTION!! (author's emphasis). Any resemblance to families living (especially the author's) is purely coincidental and all that.

Also, the word "dude" has been removed from the end of plenty of sentences for increased literary effect.

Prologue

It was suddenly summer. After the record rains. After the heavens had opened. After the eight years of drought had ended in my beloved California. After the seventeen straight days of rain. After the twenty-six days of rain in March. After all the rivers had spilled their banks. After the houses slid down the muddied mountainsides. After all the cold and the gray with your head held down as you walked along the soaked pavement. After all the days with your raincoat wrapped tightly around you, your eyes averted from the sky, the water dripping off the end of your nose. Finally, one fresh day it broke. The clouds parted, the sun appeared, and it was suddenly summer.

I was walking up in Tilden Park in the hills above Berkeley, amid the dew-drenched ferns, awash in the glory of the suddenly summer sun. From a distance there appeared a small pool of water, dark and shimmering in the light gently filtering through the trees. As

I approached the quivering pool, I realized it was brimming with tadpoles. They were plump and legless and wriggling frantically in the shallow, warm water. I knelt down and saw the high water mark the pool had once held. With each day of warm sunshine, the pool was inexorably shrinking, their fading world packing the tadpoles tighter and tighter together.

I peered deeply into the sizzling mass and saw my own reflection black. I shuddered with the tingling nausea of Existence. I saw Time running out. I saw the ruins of a wrecked world. I saw each of us alone in a shrinking pool of our own device.

However, all was not bleak. There was still hope. While the chance of rain was now remote—it never rained in California once summer began—with each day the tadpoles were transforming. Tiny legs were sprouting and a race was on to become frogs before the puddle dried up entirely. A few short yards away lay another world, a creek with water enough for them all.

Though I did not realize it as I knelt before the trembling pool of Life, suddenly that summer I was to become like the tadpoles. Circumstance would require that I spin an invisible cocoon about myself. Within its transparent walls I was to suffer the excruciating process of metamorphosis. What would become of me, I could not say. Unlike the tadpoles, my final form was undetermined. Destiny had become a gray and faded thing and Fate seemed my enemy, but Hope would lead me on.

My Hope? Love. It's all that I have left. It's all that matters. Love is my perfect ripe peach. Sweet and juicy and filled with the wealth of the season. Its tender flesh the yellow of the summer sun. Its skin blushing red with fire.

The tadpoles don't have all of that. They don't have ripe peaches driving them onward. Breaking their hearts.

One Hundred Thirty-five-Pound Hercules

Please allow me to introduce myself. I'm a man of poverty and taste. My name is Steve Reeves. What you can gather from this name, I do not know. Little, I suspect. The Oglala Sioux would at least wait until the rite of passage into manhood before bestowing the proper sobriquet. I guess that really wouldn't work nowadays. There'd be too many guys driving beer delivery trucks named "Hits with Thunder" or "Arm like a Rocket." All the computer guys driving Porsches and living in million-dollar houses would be known as "Pimply Nerd" or "He who Snivels at the Wind."

The closest I have to such a name is "College Boy." My dad likes to call me that. While this might sound as though a special honor were being granted me (the first and only in my family to graduate from college), in actuality the name is used with not a small amount of disdain. Ever since I graduated with honors from the university and ended up in low-paying service-sector jobs, "College Boy" seems to have become a code word for "Asshole."

Actually, the name "Steve Reeves" has a bit of a history. I don't know if you're aware, but Steve Reeves was the actor who portrayed Hercules in these cheesy Italian movies in the sixties. He was a Mr. Universe and built like, well, like Hercules: trim waist, huge chest, gigantic arms, strong jaw.

So, maybe you're thinking that with a name like Steve Reeves, I must be some big strapping buck. A thick-armed, football-hurling motherfucker of a son. Someone who was cut and ripped and maybe on 'roids and shit. The kind of a guy who might oil himself up before heading down to the GNC for another can of CarboLoad 2000. Someone who could tear a fucking telephone book in two.

Well, think again. I can't even tear a *TV Guide* in half. I wear glasses. Dear Old Dad's hope of a Presidential Fitness Patch for his only son was dashed by the fact that it took me all seven years of elementary school to complete a single pull up.

How about some basic facts, then:

Age: 27

Height: 5' 9"

Weight: 135

Build: Spindly

Eyesight: Corrective lenses required

Skin Color: White

Mother: Cookie-ready, yet emotionally distant

Father: A psychotic mailman

Siblings: One, Ole Sis

Diploma: College, BA in European History

Job Skills: Seemingly nonexistent

Current Position: Bagel boiler and counter dude at the BagelWorks

Income: $9,500 take home

Assets: $347.92

Address: Cottage A, Cedar Manor, Berkeley, California

Transportation: Rapidly crumbling '79 Toyota Corolla

Marital Status: Single, involved with reluctant girlfriend

Sex Life: Erratic and problematic

Friends: Three. Four, counting the reluctant girlfriend

Social Life: Minuscule and problematic

Pets: Bob, the emotionally disturbed cat

Religious Beliefs: Sketchy and opportunistic

Dreams: Late in coming, possibly dashed

Hobbies: Masturbation and delusions of grandeur

What else can I tell you? I grew up in the mythical land called Southern California. Mine was a sunny childhood filled with days rolling my Big Wheel down the innocuous sidewalks of San Diego, building sand castles on the golden beaches of La Jolla and Del Mar, attending cheery and safe public schools where I made happy artwork out of colored construction paper.

As I grew older, my lust was nurtured and my heart squashed by the dazzling bikinied beauties parading along the boardwalk from Mission to PB. My drunkenness was initiated on Boulevard Revolucion in Tijuana. My fine degree was earned at the University of California, San Diego.

You'd think that with such fair-skied beginnings, I'd be a content little soldier. That with such preparation, I'd be a happy and productive member of our Great Society. I'm not. I'm a malcontent. A misfit. The American Dream continues to elude me.

Why? Perhaps it is my fate. I remain my father's son. The son of a mailman. It was *he* who planted an evil seed deep within me. It was *he* who nurtured it. It is *I* who will have to dispose of it.

Son of a Mailman

Mom and Dad had been turning the screws for quite some time to get me to come down to San Diego and attend my sister's wedding. For some reason, my presence was required. Why, I don't know. It's not like my sister and I really spoke to one another, but after Dad bitterly offered to pay for the flight from San Francisco, there was no way I could refuse.

San Diego. Strange things happen to me whenever I return. I'm like a tourist in a strange and horrific climate. It's as though I'm suddenly at 12,000 feet and can't get enough air, or I'm in some thick, wet jungle feeling the first suggestion of an upcoming bout with malaria.

The endless tract homes, the listless smog, Dad's infinite complaints, the countless minimalls, the blinding summer heat hammering upon the lifeless pavement—it all combines to suck the very marrow out of my soul. In the Great Southland, a person's spirit desiccates in a matter of minutes. It dries up as quickly as the chaparral in June, and like the chaparral, one's entire being sits silent, dry, and dead and on the constant verge of bursting into flames and consuming all in its wake.

This San Diego Soul Death is one of the reasons I moved up to Berkeley. That, and to put enough miles between me and my parents to both preempt any unannounced visits on their part and require nothing more than seasonal holiday visits of my own.

And now The Wedding. It was billed as an All-Time Great Family Event. A crowning moment of Glory. Never mind that Ole Sis and her man, Doug, had been living together for a couple of years or that Ole Sis was swollen with child in, this, her fifth month. At long last my sister was finally getting married and Mom was practically beaming with her ever-present benign smile. It was a slight variation on the ever-present benign smile Mom wore during family gatherings at Thanksgiving and Christmas, a delicate twist to the ever-present benign smile she wore when Dad foamed and hissed at her and called her an idiot. It was more or less the same ever-present benign smile she wore the day I graduated from college—*my* last great day in the sun.

The service at Her Lady of Amazing Grace Church in El Cajon was both endless and painful (my family is very uncomfortable in churches and enters them about as often as a wandering band of Gypsy Satan worshipers), but somehow I survived the whole affair: the deadening, 104-degree heat; the sickly, treacly strains of the folk guitar strummer; the mumbo jumbo, New Agey vows delivered by the priest who came garbed in a flowing purple robe affair that I think he picked up at an Artist Formerly Known as Prince yard sale; my keen embarrassment when Dad marveled at the miracle of

9

life in Ole Sis's womb by announcing in an overly loud voice, "Jesus H. Christ, she looks so fat in that gown."

The rings were exchanged, the bouquet tossed, the birdseed hurled, and off we headed to the reception at my parents' house. Dad was once again saving money on Mom's cheap labor.

I need a drink! is my first thought when we arrive at my parents' house and I head straight for the spare fridge in the family room that is always loaded with cheap beer. My family is the kind that needs an entire extra refrigerator just to hold all the beer required to keep family members from coming to actual blows. (Or maybe it was all the beer that got everyone worked up to begin with. We'll never know because there will never be a day without the spare fridge loaded with lots of cheap beer.)

As I crack open what would be the first of far too many Coors (Dear Old Dad's beloved brew) Mom comes up to me, weeping.

"That bastard," she sobs ("Bastard" was Mom's pet name for Dad. I liked "Asshole," while Ole Sis used the more tender "Jerk"), "I can't believe he called your sister 'fat.' At her wedding." She looks at me imploringly.

I make a feeble attempt at comforting her, but since I was mostly deprived of any physical contact for the first eighteen years of my life, I'm ill-equipped (my family approached touching each other with the same relish most people reserve for colon irrigation—it's supposed to be good for you, but nobody's very comfortable with the idea).

I still can't believe that Ole Sis married a mailman of her own. Not after Dad. You'd think she'd've known better. Mailmen are no good. It's no accident them killing each other all the time. I remember growing up and waiting (well, hoping actually) for the day when the knock would come on *our* door and police officers, surrounded by a throng of reporters, would regretfully inform us that Dad had taken one of his many guns to work and slaughtered numerous coworkers. After the revelation about Santa Claus, it was one of the things I most looked forward to at Christmastime: that this would be the holiday season Dad finally went to jail.

But there's no making sense of Ole Sis. Despite our sharing identical genetic material, Sis and I couldn't be less alike. Except for a three-year period commencing on her seventeenth birthday when she became Maniacal Drug Swallowing Slut-Tramp (a couple of ill-advised tattoos are the only permanent mark from those days) Ole Sis has been the model of Stepfordian delight. She revels in the comfortable coziness of her cog-in-the-machine suburban slow-death dreams, while I am often unable to even scrounge up a date. *My* wedding guest is an alienation with the gravitational pull of the planet Jupiter. But, it's all good. Soon we'll be arguing over Sis's Republican politics and my lack of a decent job.

The groom's family seems a little ill at ease with the screaming that my family passes off as conversation. They're standing off to one side of the living room looking like a bunch of settlers circling their wagon train awaiting the first attack by the Comanches. They mainly consist of ex-Navy men; their sun-shriveled, wraithlike wives; and their blockheaded, probably racist children. Luckily, they all seem to drink, so everything should go well.

There's a commotion in the kitchen. It seems Gramma has tossed aside her walker and has commandeered the stove. Gramma is . . . I don't know. No one is still alive who can testify to Gramma's age. She claims to have met Hitler. Say ninety. Something in Mom's food preparation smacks of the convenient to Gramma's Old World eyes. She's digging around in the potato salad and doesn't like what she sees. Gramma blames the Jews.

If Gramma were at all mobile, she'd probably get in a lot more trouble. Fortunately, she's very ancient and can only move about with the aid of her walker or a brace she wears on her right leg that goes up to mid-thigh.

I hear Dad calling me. I've been avoiding him, of course, but now he needs me. Maybe he misses me now that I live so far away. Maybe he's reaching out to his only boy. I hear words I know very well. The one request I've always been able to fulfill.

"Hey, Steve! Gemme a beer!"

Dad is in the den polishing one of his many handguns. On the table lie gun cleaning supplies, a stack of *Cheri* magazines, and about fifty bulk mail samples of minty green Plax (Dad feels stealing bulk mail samples are something of a letter carrier's birthright). I have an almost genetic-level urge to pocket a few of them myself.

I hand Dad a can of Coors and crack open one for myself. He slams his into a fucking grubby foam cozy that's had the advertisement long ago worn away, replaced with a grimy black discoloration in the vague shape of Dad's left hand. My brain begins to fog as I desperately clutch my can of Coors, sans cozy.

Dad continues to polish in silence. I see the deep furrows in his brow that run up to near the top of his bald dome. Furrows that can only mean one thing: I've fucked something up again. I'm fairly certain a lecture about the troublesome juxtaposition of my college degree and my high-powered career in the bagel industry is forthcoming.

Dad begins his speech but quickly goes apoplectic, fizzing and foaming like the rotten beers he constantly swills. "Ecck. Acchh! Clckglcch!!" I'm not sure exactly what he's trying to say, but that's what it sounds like. Something about "West Point this" and "Law school that." A "With those grades," is followed by a "God-damned bagel shop!" It's all peppered with lots of "Christs!" whom Dad always represents as "Sweet Limpin' " or "Jesus H."

My lack of a braggable job has recently replaced my lack of athletic prowess in Dear Old Dad's Disappointment Book. He's got it all worked out, you know. All the times I've let him down. This seems to be a culmination of sorts. The only shame remaining is for me to take up homosexuality.

Besides being a mailman, I think part of Dad's problem is his size. He's stunningly short. I had to move 600 miles away for the proper perspective to realize the scale of his tininess. It was only through some miraculous genetic benevolence on my Mom's part that I somehow reached the towering height of sixty-nine inches (really, the bare minimum for walking down America's streets without being labeled "dwarfish").

Dad wasn't so lucky. While he appeared huge in my childhood (arriving home each day in his postal uniform, appearing to my elementary-school eyes to be of the same terrorizing mood and size as Godzilla, tearing open cans of Coors rather than Tokyo city buses), it turns out he barely notched in at five foot four. Sadly, what Dad lacks in size, he makes up for in toxic personality and an extensive gun collection.

As Dad continues with his rant, I again try to accept the fact that we will never be close. Oh, I've tried. In an attempt to get to know Dad a little better, I've become something of an amateur scholar on Postal Revenge Slayings. Did you know that since 1983 there have been thirty-six killings in thirteen separate incidents? This isn't even counting David Berkowitz, the Son of Sam.

In fact, I've developed an entire theory on my Dad's psychological depravity based upon Postal Worker Revenge Killers. Unfortunately, no one will listen.

Dad continues to polish the weapons. "Sweet limpin' Christ! How can you just work at a bagel shop?"

"I don't know."

"You're not even Jewish."

"It's just a job."

Dad then busts out with his favorite rhetorical: "What the hell is wrong with you?"

I shrug.

He emits an incredulous grunt and shakes his head.

Mom yells that dinner is ready.

At one point, after dinner and before the cake cutting, Dad, into his sixteenth Coors, decides it would be a good idea for the men to go out back for some target practice.

We've all had a bit too much to drink, and Mom protests the unlocking of the ammo boxes, but Dad waves this off as the whining of womenfolk as Doug, Dad, and I head to the backyard with a Colt .45, a Baretta 92f nine, a Smith & Wesson .22 revolver, fifty rounds of .45 and nine ammo, a box of 100 .22 long rifle hollow points, and a can of Coors to a man.

Doug, the new son-in-law, the latest mailman in the clan, seems rather quiet and a bit nervous (I'm giving him three years before he mows down some coworkers with an assault rifle).

"Now, he can't do much right," Dad brags enthusiastically about me, "but he can shoot like a sonuvabitch."

Doug nods and opens his can of Coors. The target is a fat Valencia hanging off the orange tree. A tree, incidentally, that seems to thrive under Dad's annual Yuletide barrage of gunfire, each season's harvest greater than the last.

Doug goes first, and he misses completely, but he shows an immediate ease with the handgun that I imagine is second nature to all letter carriers.

"Okay, too bad," Dad champs as he licks his lips and takes careful aim. BAM! BAM! BAM! The Colt is fearsome and resounding compared to the Baretta. His last shot grazes the orange, but leaves it swinging on the branch.

"Damn! All right, your shot, College Boy." Dad quickly glances in my general direction (my family wasn't big on eye contact, either, and Dad and I had somehow avoided it altogether for over twenty years).

I take my spot and raise the long-barreled S&W. The mailmen had made the mistake of choosing the loud, well-hung guns, leaving me with the more accurate weapon.

Tick! It sounds like a cap gun, but the first shot rips a hole in the orange, lower right center.

"Check it out, gentlemen," I gloat as we walk up to examine the badly wounded citrus.

"Mmmm," Dad grumbles.

Toward the end of the evening, after everyone except Mom and Gramma were quite liquored up, Doug comes up to me, a bit nervous, a mite tentative, slurring slightly. We nod to each other and flash the smile that men like to use. The one where the ends of the mouth turn *down,* like we're bucking up for the long piece of work that lay ahead, the tough job we must now perform: conversation.

"Hiya," Doug grunts.

"Hey, congratulations," I say. "If you ever need verification on any childhood stories of Ole Sis, just ask me."

I say this as a joke, not that it was so very funny, but Doug takes it seriously with a look on his face that says he appreciates this offer, but secretly he's worried, possibly, for my sanity. All I can think is, yeah, but *you're* the mailman, buddy.

"Ya know, I got some friends in the PO," Doug says, sipping his Coors. "Up in Frisco."

I hate when anyone calls it "Frisco" and am now sure the marriage will be a success because anything I hated, Ole Sis loved.

"I could maybe put in a good word for you," Doug offers, as though I am suddenly in desperate need of becoming a mailman.

"Cool," I say and take a good long swig off my Coors. Doug does likewise.

"It's great job," Doug continues, "a career, really. Good pay. Some of the supes are real assholes, but I figure that's the way it is in any job. Ya know?"

"Sure."

"Yeah, the Post Office . . ." Doug gets a far-off look on his face that might be described as either misty-eyed or that of a man about to make a very difficult, very permanent decision. "I'm no College Boy like yourself, but I got a steady job, benefits, paid vacation, house, wife, kid on the way, and, one day, retirement, ya know?"

The picture in my head makes me want to scream. I now need to strap on the mask from Gramma's tank and breathe pure oxygen. They just didn't get it. None of them got it. I wasn't San Diego material. I just wasn't mailman material.

After another twelve hours of rollicking good fun with my family, I couldn't wait to get back to the Bay Area. Mom and Dear Old Dad took me to the airport. Just as we were leaving, Dad, in his infinite uncomfortability with any emotion except that of rage and blame (the quintessential slaughtering mailman except he didn't have the guts for it and sometimes I think that's what I hated most about him: he could talk the talk, but he couldn't pull the trigger), handed over to me with astronomical difficulty a package that took me a moment to recognize. The triangular brown leather satchel.

"Here, take this," he said, his eyes glued to the floor. He shoved it in my hands and then turned away as soon as he said (as though he had identified another character flaw of mine), "You always liked it."

I looked at the package. I knew it was one of Dad's two Colt .45s, and I smiled sardonically because it was the revolver that I coveted, not the Colt.

"Well, open it," he said angrily.

I unzipped it and pulled out first the clip and then the pistol. "Gee, thanks."

The handing off of the gun (I guess my Dad's warped idea of fatherhood and what that might entail) took on a sinister air in the silence, Dad looking at his shoes (his usual spite momentarily replaced by an aggrieved uneasiness), Mom putting on her coat, and my mind flashing with images of me shooting him dead.

We left for the airport and the drive took a lifetime. An interminable and excruciating lifetime. As I suffered in the back, Dad groused about something, anything, it didn't matter, he had bile and hate to release. Bile and hate which, I guess, required an audience, and Mom and I trapped in the car proved perfect.

"Christ! This weather. It's not gonna rain. They said it's gonna rain. They don't know," or "This rain! Christ! It's June. This weather's pathetic!"

Thankfully it was only a twenty-minute drive. After cursing at a couple of traffic lights that didn't respond quite to his liking and directing a particularly potent invective at an unfortunate in front of us who failed to respond to a green light as though he were in a drag race, we somehow made it to the airport without Dad directing his usual personal attack on Mom.

As the car pulled up to the passenger unloading zone, I had just reached the stage in my usual fantasy wherein I crack Dear Old Dad on the side of his head. Pap! Just crack him a high hard one on his impossibly long ear. Pap! A whole world is destroyed and a whole new one created. A lightning jab to the side of Dad's dome could have greatly altered our present relationship, but I didn't have the stomach for it. What if we became closer?

Dad performed his usual up close and personal method of saying good-bye by telling Mom, "We better get going, huh? I don't wanna get stuck in traffic."

Mom actually busted out with a hug, one of about three or four she issued each year. She hugged me, secretly handed me some cash, and shot me a look and I had a brief flash of clarity or paranoia (I'm not sure which, you never are) that she was a secret captive and required liberation. That I should send for the authorities or, better yet, shoot Dad with the gun.

San Francisco. I missed it whenever I left, all Big Citied up like nothing else on the coast. The Bridges.

The Fog. The 600 miles of distance it puts between me and my family. Cool Berkeley late at night when the trees seem to engulf the darkened streets up Northside. I even missed work for a mad instant.

And Rachel. When I watched Ole Sis jam some wedding cake into Doug's face, as I saw a glimpse of the Love she felt, I thought about Rachel. She's my girlfriend. Sort of. I seem to like her best whenever I'm away. What's with that? It's almost love. At least it feels like it is, sometimes. Is that enough?

I remembered last year when we first started going out and we went to the City to eat fresh crab. We took BART and then a bus to Fisherman's Wharf. Crabs are cheaper in Chinatown, but more fun to buy at the Wharf. Especially those first crabs of the season, when the sky is gray and winter cold.

The crab was tasty good. Damn tasty good and succulent and sweet and salty like the ocean. Rachel and I sat below Ghiradelli Square on a wall down by the water and ate that crab with a sourdough baguette while the seagulls wheeled and squawked in the sky above. We pulled the meat out of the thin orange shells, we carefully picked the sweet flesh from the body, we sucked the tiniest morsels from the smallest legs, we licked our fingers, and laughed as a seagull tried to sneak up from behind to steal some baguette but only came away with the bag.

We finished our crab and Rachel grabbed the back of my neck and pulled me to her for a sweet and salty kiss and we licked our lips and scoured the shiny white paper amid the scraps that was once a Dungeness crab and found no more.

One crab is never enough, but then neither is two, so it's best to leave it at one and lick the last bits off your fingers and lips and remark at what a wonderful crab it was. How it was the best crab ever as the first crab of the season often is. So head down to the Wharf and bring your girl and buy that crab. Get a hot one out of the steaming, stainless steel vat, and the man will crack it for you. Get some bread and maybe a cold Anchor Steam and sit down by the water and throw the last bits of bread into the sky to the legions of seagulls who cry and circle about and never miss. They're like circus acrobats when it comes to that bread.

It's with such thoughts running through my mind that the plane touches down at SFO into the fog cool welcome of San Francisco. I love the sight of her, great city that she be, and I can't wait to get back to the tree-lined sweet streets of Berkeley to resume my now beloved Life (Life that was all shit and angst-ridden before my trip to Ole Sis's wedding, now a jewel rediscovered upon my return).

It's eight o'clock at night with light aplenty in June, but no sun, all gray, and Brady's there to meet me and we swing down into the Mission for some tacos and then to a bar to shoot some pool with a couple of boys from down Michoacán way. I could hardly wait to see Rachel.

Rachel: I nearly allowed myself the heady release of love's intoxication as Brady lined up a shot, and when he sank that shot and the Michoacán boys tapped their cues on the floor in approval, well, life was wonderful and good and would do for right now. I was practically happy and content.

Then came the next day.

Drunk before Noon

"What'll it be, son?" old man Mack asked as I walked up to the bar in the seedy darkness of The Yukon, a working-class dive down San Pablo way.

"A pint of Redhook, please," I ordered, sat down on a stool, and set down my plastic Hefty bag filled with bagels.

"There you are." Mack slid the pint my way. "That'll be three twenty-five."

I reached into my pocket and pulled out a roll of bills and peeled a twenty off the top. "Here you go. . . . Uh, would you like a bagel?" I asked rather tentatively.

"Huh?" Mack furrowed his brow as he took my money and I noticed his eyes dart toward the baseball bat I knew he stored behind the bar.

"A bagel," I tried to reassure him. "I got 'em from work."

"Oh. Uh, why not?" Mack smiled a bit nervously as he handed me my change. "Whaddaya got?"

"Let's see." I rummaged through the bag. "Pretty

21

much everything: plain, poppy seed, garlic, rye, blue-
berry . . ."

"Got any onion bagels?"

*He wants my onion bagels, the fucker. Those are
my favorites!*

"Umm . . . sure." I tried to smile and handed Mack
a couple of onion bagels and cracked open my newspaper. It was 10:30 and the bright July sun shot
through the open top half of The Yukon's Dutch door
and glanced blindingly off the bar. I moved to an empty
table in a dark corner.

I took my seat in the corner, in the cool, dark light.
Summer splendid outside, but that was another world,
some other time. I took my seat too stunned to know.
I wondered, *Could it all happen so quickly? Would it
all happen so quickly?* But it had, so I guess it does and
there I was: fucked. My world was shattered. Everything was gone. All that I hated was now gone.

I sat in the back of that bar, in the weird light of
bright midday now crashing in, the sunlight creating an
impenetrable wall of yellow brilliance at the door. I felt
there was no escape, that I was a dark mole in the bowels of Satan's Bar and Grill silently viewing the lost souls
collected that day.

The place was nearly deserted. An old alcoholic on
Social Security nursing a glass of cheap draft, two blue-
collars in repairman jumpsuits and tan working boots,
that white-haired lady who likes to play liar's dice. The
jukebox sat silent. The pool table empty.

I tried to read the paper as I greedily gulped down
that first pint. I tried to worry about the team and
whether or not they could take the pennant. I tried to
lose myself in the adult movie ads extolling the virtues
of lap dancers with names like Jasmine and Goldie, but
it was a no go. You see, I'm not usually in a bar trying

to get drunk at 10:30 in the morning, but today was special.

It began the same as usual. I headed out the door, late as usual, and quickly walked the eight blocks down Shattuck Avenue to the BagelWorks and my special job that I love, oh, so much.

I stepped into the doughy warmth of the kitchen. Jose was there. He had the big Hobart mixer working and he was tending a steaming vat of bagels. The coffeepot was on, the funny morning radio show played, Jose said "Buenas dias" and "Como estas?" and I did likewise. Betsy, the counter girl, would arrive shortly.

It's kinda nice in the morning, the three of us telling stories, working quietly. The shop is warm and smells of baking. We eat warm bagels and drink coffee in the early morning light.

Yeah, but that's all over now. Those days are gone forever. The boss, one Russell Shorter, saw to that this morning. I knew it was trouble when he called me into his cluttered office first thing this morning.

"Late again, Reeves?" He leaned back in his chair, feet up on the desk, classical music station on the radio, hands behind his head like he's somebody important when, in reality, he's just a stupid bagel monger. "What's that, third time this pay period?"

I mumbled a combination apology/excuse along the lines of "I, uh . . . well, er . . . I don't think . . ."

"Yeah, that's your problem," Shorter interrupted. "You just don't think. Do you . . . College Boy?"

I really wasn't in the mood for one of his patented weekly fits since I'd already spilled a vat of salmon schmear all over the kitchen floor, not to mention the unmentioned personal tragedies pounding on my brain's door that morning.

But Shorter was already rambling on incoherently, his arms flailing, tiny pockets of foam forming at the corners of his lamprey mouth.

"Uh, I better get going," I said. "Lotta work to do. Lotta work."

Shorter was now scratching the top of his narrow head and then carefully examining the dredgings of his fingernails. He pondered my words as though he were retarded and then whiffed his fingers to further ID their findings. I guess the aromatherapy was not in my favor because the next thing he said, cutting short his usual Monday morning lecture, was, "No, there's not a lotta work for you, Reeves. I've had it with you. You're fired."

He tossed me an envelope of cash and leaned back in his chair again. His hands, their work completed, returned behind his head and a wry little smile formed on his face. A smirk, perhaps. A gloat.

I was stunned. It's not that I liked the job, but it had always been my dream to one day quit—without notice. Perhaps even drive up for my last paycheck in a stretch limo with a couple of porno actresses. Damn.

"Well," I informed Shorter, nodding my head, eager to wreck his little world. "I ain't cleanin' up that schmear then. You can forget the schmear . . . and I'm taking some bagels with me, too."

I had more than the bagels by the time I walked (ran, technically) out that back door for the last time, Shorter screaming at me with threats of police action and the like. I had macked not only the biggest bag of the best bagels (Oh, how I hoped to somehow pack that bag with at least six months worth of morning bagels), but had lined the lower reaches with tubs of cream cheese, sheets of smoked salmon, and sixers of these cream sodas that cost like a buck a bottle, but they're the best damn sodas and certainly worth trying to steal. Especially from some crappy job where they just fired you out of nowhere.

That's how I ended up at The Yukon at 10:30 in the morning on a Monday. My world had come down to this: jacked heistings of former bagel bosses. My haul amounted to $249 in pay and $150 worth of bagel shop products. (I had scored big on the smoked Nova Scotia salmon, but many of the cream sodas had been confiscated by Shorter at the back door amid some anger and some shame and the warning to never show my face there again. Oh, and to forget about any sort of a good job reference. That was apparently out.)

Suddenly, intricate scenarios began to form and take shape like devilish ice crystals deep within my brain. The Boss is tied to a chair. The chair is bolted to the floor. I've got a device mounted to his narrow head that keeps him from moving or closing his mouth or eyes, which are pried wide open. Jose and Betsy have been sent home. I've locked the front door to the 'Works and turned the sign to read Closed. I have at my disposal a variety of power tools and corrosive solvents, flammable liquids and blowtorches. And, of course, my new Colt .45 Mark IV. Unless I receive some answers, some sort of satisfaction, I will have no choice but to blast a couple of fat .45 slugs into his skinny knees. Until he explains how he dared fire me, I will continue to use my Black & Decker minidrill on his squirming tongue. If I don't hear some tearful begging for forgiveness, I'll be forced to apply the whizzing circular saw to the top of his dome—bloody chunks of scalp flying everywhere.

Hmmm, my glass appears empty.

Pint Two

Yeah, well, fuck that job, anyway. I hated it. And I hated that idiot Shorter even more.

Suddenly, I felt a great weight lifting. I took a long drink from that second Redhook and was absolutely and marvelously fueled by the bitter ale, by what I *now* took to be my great good fortune at having been fired. Thank you, Shorter. You did me a favor, you sorry old fuck.

Anything seemed possible. The loathsome yolk of another life-draining job had been jettisoned. I was freed from the tar pit trap of the BagelWorks and could begin my new Life as an Artist. Artist with a capital *A*. My only problem was a lack of any obvious prodigy-level talent of any kind as well as a rather nebulous, half-baked conception of what, exactly, being an Artist meant. My notion of an Artist was a romantic one (as well as being probably completely false): brooding writers smoking cigarettes at cafés or flying down the road à la Kerouac. Soulful rock stars screaming their very life into a microphone. Idiots who put broken, upside-down toilet bowls in the Museum of Modern Art. My main fantasy being: Artist on Holiday, or Artist Getting Hella Money, or Artist Getting Hella Pussy. It was *never* Artist Hard at Work.

So what is it I'm getting at? Namely, that perhaps Dear Old Dad was right. I'm a good-for-nothing punk.

But I took another long drink and thought, *Fuck him!* Perhaps a new day *was* dawning. I downed another quaff and fell into a dizzingly delicious state of High Anxiety. Yes, it's all falling into place, don't you see? An old world is being destroyed and from its ashes will be delivered a new life, full-formed and gasping for breath.

Yes, my firing today, coming as it did right upon the heels of my breakup with Rachel, is surely a sign. I am a reptile shedding my skin of old, emerging moist and eager.

Yeah, Rachel. Dear Rachel. Is it really appropriate to break up by leaving a message on the answering machine? I don't believe so, but I have no time to await Miss Manners's answer.

I got home late last night and it felt good to be back at Cedar Manor. Since I'd been gone for three days, I saw that my answering machine was burgeoning with three whole messages.

BEEP!

Yo dude. Yo dude. Yo, yo, yo. I'm down at The Congo. Dude, it's crawlin' with bitches. Where's your lazy ass at, dude! YEAH!

BEEP!

This is Mom. I just wanted to call to see that you got back safe. It was so nice that you came down. The wedding was nice and I'm glad there was nice weather for your visit. Call me. Bye.

BEEP!

Uh, it's me, Rachel, um, I know you're down in San Diego and all, but, like, well, I just don't think this is working out, Steve. You know? I'm becoming a vegan and all and you like Green Day and, well, I don't know. Look, I just don't think we should see each other anymore, ya know? Sorry. . . . Oh! Can I get my Phish CDs back?

I tried calling her, thinking it was some joke or some sort of mistake, but no one was home. Luckily, since I was fired some eight hours later, I had the free time on my hands to track her ass down where she worked, at Café Ole, the trendy cafe/tapas bar.

The two of us sat across from each other. For some

27

perverse reason, I never loved her more than right then as she toyed coyly with the tiny spoon in her cappuccino, looking up at me through her bangs of fine, auburn hair. Those deep blue eyes. Her fine, delicate hands. That ripe rose of a mouth. And from that lovely flower issued forth the tender words, "Look, I've gotta get back to work."

It came out that she just couldn't see me anymore, that it was over. I was stunned and asked why, but it was as though she were speaking some new and foreign language. She said something about seeing somebody else and no, it was nobody I knew. His name was Rich, if I had to know. How I loved her then, when it became clear that she was no longer mine. The fact that she would never again fuck me made all our differences vanish into the foggy sky.

Well, she said "Sorry" about nineteen times and that it wasn't my fault and she offered to pay for the coffees like that would fucking help. I swallowed back the gigantic lump, the rotten chunk of love lost's coal that had grown in my throat and she gave me a hug and kissed me on the cheek like she was my aunt or something. It was a kiss of death. There was no denying the cold leftover feeling of that icy peck. She was suddenly a psychopath. Her eyes had gone cold and fish dead. Rachel.

But she hoped we could be friends, you know. I smiled and said, "Sure." Instantly, one part of my brain worked on winning her back while the other imagined the great and painful price she would pay for her treachery.

We walked our separate ways and after a couple of steps I heard her call my name. I imagined she'd had second thoughts. That we would run toward each other and into the comfort of each other's arms. Reunited. All is forgiven.

"Steve," she called, "you didn't happen to bring those Phish CDs with you, did you?"

I turned and walked away. I felt like I was falling. Like I had asthma. It was late morning, and the fog was beginning to break up, but suddenly it felt very cold out and I wondered, should I simply smash the Phish CDs or actually go to the trouble of melting them?

Oh, sweet Rachel. Oh, my auburn-haired darling of lovely long limbs. Oh, my lost lithe lover. Oh . . . fuck you!

I'm not gonna weep into my beer over her black heart. Not today! I'm a Man, god damn it! After draining my second pint I've got my balls strapped in place. They've become weighty, the size of oranges. Testosterone races through my system like a Wyoming cowpoke fresh in town after thirty days on the Sante Fe Trail.

Let's get back to Shorter. I'm thinking the Royal Oak, Michigan, Post Office, November 14, 1991. Thomas McIlvane, part-time postal clerk who's worked his way up from postal custodian, is in deep shit. He's been fired for time card tampering. A trained kick boxer, Tommy walks into the Royal Oak PO—armed with a sawed-off Ruger semiauto .22 rifle—to have a little "chat" with the supervisors who done him wrong. He had told coworkers that if he lost his job, he'd make the Oklahoma postal tragedy look like a tea party, but he falls far short of Patrick Sherrill's record and only kills four supervisors before capping himself.

I can just see Shorter. I've still got him tied to the chair and he's bleeding pretty badly about the head and his tongue is kinda fucked up. I'm now dressed in full postal uniform, my mail bag stuffed with bagels and

29

smoked salmon. Instead of the Ruger mini-14, I'm brandishing my new Colt .45 in Shorter's face.

"I'll give you back your job. Please, please don't kill me," Shorter blubbers.

"And a raise?" I walk cockily around the chair gently tapping him on the noggin with the barrel of my pistol.

"Anything. Yes!"

"I don't know . . . Russell," I answer. He would never allow us to call him by his first name. "May I call you Russell?"

"Yes! Yes, just let me go."

"I just don't know, Russell. How 'bout *Rusty?* Can I call you *Rusty?*"

"Yes! Just please, please let me go . . ."

"I'm so sorry. I'd like to. I really would, but you're simply too disgusting for sympathy." And then, realizing he's just another asshole boss, I take a straight razor and remove a three-inch strip of flesh from along his jawline.

"Arrgghh!! Awklckcl!" He gurgles with pain.

I hate work. But hey, look at me! I'm unemployed and that thought—coming as it did right upon the heels of the torture sequence—left me quite satisfied, with merely the thirst for another beer.

I approached the bar for my third pint. Old Mildred had replaced Mack at the bar. I ordered a Sierra Nevada Pale. I was now more than a bit randy and I eyed the rather worn and ragged barmaid—she's a bit past harvest time—with a sailor's lust.

They've got this other girl. This pretty young thing. Crystal. She's not on duty right now. They save her juicy shit for the night shifts when the rowdy frat boys sometimes come down from campus to slum.

Pint Three

As I returned to my seat with my beer, I'm completely in love with Crystal. She's the sweetest thing. A fine young girl all legs and lean arms, but soft shouldered with an open smile and the palest green eyes that look right through you. She could cut my heart in two with those eyes, but she doesn't mean nothin' by it. I wish she was here right now.

But she wasn't. It was good old Mildred and as I took a good long guzzle of ale, I loved Mildred, too. She worked hard and her life seemed hard and the hard years had maybe gotten the better of her, but she was a hard worker in the worker's sense of a working class . . . working all the time. Hard.

Fuck all the rich assholes up in the hills with their superior airs and their smug little Volvo station wagons. Working class sounded so good right then. Nothing fancy. Simple pleasures. To what more could I ever aspire? I imagined Mildred with a contentedness that I would never possess, but what if it were really a resignation to which I never wanted to fall victim?

My brain began to glow with alcohol warmth. I looked out the door to the yellow light of the street and felt content and safe in the darkness of The Yukon. There was something incredibly uplifting about my happy beer buzz and seeing the bright light of before noon out that door. And me, out of work, yet with a wad of cash rolled up in my pocket. A big bag of assorted bagels by my side. And smoked salmon to boot!

The excitement made me horny. I near throbbed as I gripped the thick base of my pint of ale. "Grog, mateys!" I yelled in my head. "Ayes and Arghs all around!" There's something thrillingly British about slamming back pints at midday. I felt the teeth rot in my head and had a sudden appetite for meat pies. An unexpected sadness for Lady Di overcame me, and I wanted to fuck her right then. I saw the romance in an eye patch and wished I had my own pet parrot sitting on my shoulder. I rued the loss of Empire.

I'm going to have to start drinking earlier in the future, I decided. No more of this waiting around till nighttime. Daytime drinking was a workingman's pleasure I found meaty and welcome. Yeah, so I'm a little drunk? What of it? And so I'm out of a job? And so my woman left me for a guy named Rich? And so it's only five minutes until noon? Five minutes to *All My Children*, man. Not that I watch soaps, but now I could, don't you see? That's the advantage of unemployment and no social life. An entire world of daytime TV is open to me. Marvel at its delights.

I eyed a calender on the wall of an utterly breathtaking swimsuited beauty. She's okay, but it's Christy Turlington that I love. She's from around here, you know. I hope one day to meet her. Oh, Christy.

My heart ached emptily. My crotch throbbed with desire. I would've happily gone home with a warm, overripened melon right then. And then I remembered Oreos! And, Yes! It's a date! Nothing would stop me from buying a five and a half ounce box of Oreos at the 7-Eleven on the way home. Fuck it! It's Safeway and a pound-and-a-quarter bag! And why not?! It was decided, and I could hardly wait. I'd eat the whole fucking bag if I wanted.

I drained the third pint and it came to me. *Scarface*. 1983. Directed by Brian DiPalma. Screenplay by Oliver Stone. The scene in which Tony Montana has gone to deliver the money to the Colombians and it's a setup.

I now have Shorter handcuffed to the shower curtain rod. He's bleeding pretty bad about the face and head, but that's what he gets for firing me. For fucking with me! You little monkey!

Shorter's rambling on incoherently like he always used to do at work. My Poulan eighteen-inch gas-powered chain saw sits at the ready, sputtering malevolently. I've got all the time in the world.

"I tole you. Don' fuck wi' me you li'l monkey. Don' you ever fuck wi' me," I say calmly.

"You bastard. You're insane!" Shorter's blubbering.

"You should'a thaw abow tha' when you juan gimme time off to see Nirvana and now Cobain's dead. How 'bout tha'? How you like tha'?"

"What do you want? I'll give you anything you want."

"What do I juan? I juan you to say hello to my li'l fren." And with my trusty Poulan, I give him a case of chapped lips that even Carmex can't repair. BRRRRZZZZ!!!

Pint Four

An old guy came in, sat down at the bar, and chatted up old Mildred. He was a crusty old gentleman. His nose was as red and dimpled as a ripe strawberry. There was something about the slow grandeur of his movements, the alcoholic pallor of his skin, the peach-colored polyester sansabelt slacks hitched high on his waist. He filled me with an inspiring sadness.

What a tough old bird. They don't make guys like that anymore. Look at those slacks, the dress shoes with the spit shine, those big, meaty, bleached-haired forearms. I walked up to get my fourth beer and decided to strike up a conversation with my new pal.

"Hiya," I grunted a nod in his general direction.

"Howya doin', young man?" the old geezer said, extending a hand. His forearm was Popeye-like and bore a tattoo of a snake wrapped around a dagger. "Jack Lazzeri."

"Steve. Steve Reeves." We shook. "You can call me Reeves."

"Hmmm." Jack stroked his chin. "Where do I know that name from?"

I tried to think up something quick before he remembers the Movie Star Steve Reeves and feels obliged to mention how little, in fact, I'm built like Hercules: "You seem like a cantankerous old alky." "Is your presence the future I have to look forward to?" "What's with your nose?"—but none of these will do.

"My Dad was in the Marines," I somehow blurted out of nowhere like some idiot.

"Marines?! I'm a Navy man!" Jack practically yelled and seemed genuinely angry. *This* is why I almost never talk to people.

"Well . . ." I was thinking fast, and I thought of Grampa who had been at Pearl Harbor as a twenty-three-year-old Navy machinist. "My grandfather was in the Navy. Pearl Harbor. He died in the war."

"Pearl Harbor?" Jack calmed down a bit. "You don't say. I was on the USS *Limatour*. Battle of the Java Sea, they called it."

"Were you under attack?"

"Under attack?! The goddamned ship went down!"

"Jesus."

"We were in the water for eight hours. I was only nineteen at the time." Jack glared at me as though it were *I* who ordered the attack on his ship. "Six hundred and fifty-eight crewmen and only 126 of us made it back."

"You were in the water?"

"Hell yes! The lieutenant ordered everybody out of the raft who wasn't wounded or injured. It was night. Dark as all hell. We were grabbing anything that floated by: Medicine cabinets, mess tables, benches."

"Were there sharks?"

Jack thought back, he drifted back a half century before my very eyes, back to the cold, black Java Sea and he nodded his head as he took up his glass of Scotch, neat, and said, "Sharks."

"I'm gonna get you a bagel," I slurred.

"Huh? What's that?" Jack looked concerned.

"You just wait there. I'm gonna get you a nice bagel."

After Old Mack defused the tense situation over the bagel misunderstanding, I took my seat and a drink off my fourth pint, an Anchor Steam because I live in a beerman's paradise and I love my new friend Jack Lazzeri, despite him calling me a Commie pinko fag over my offer of a bagel. We're Americans goddamn it! I love this man and want to champion his cause. Into my fourth pint I'd walk to the ends of the world for this old, white-haired patriot.

I marveled at the Wonder and Beauty of Life. I grew up in the sheltered and comfy cradle of the U.S. of A. A land this great patriot at the bar nearly gave his life for!

I felt the hot blush of shame as I realize the Easy Life that lay at my fingertips. I almost wept at the Sadness of Life because it is in an easy chair with belly full that one may weep the most delicious tears of all. Yet all the opportunity, all the creature comforts, it wasn't enough, motherfucker! My Mounds-barred, skateboarded boytime. My complete safety and snack-filled childhood. It all seemed a small fortune to my full-grown yet wrecked adulthood.

I was again a miserable and horny fuck. The patriotism seemed to have worn off rather quickly. Did I tell you how much I love Oreos? They're one of America's great achievements, along with cars, baseball, hamburgers, and sinsemilla. These are our great things.

But I was getting to that point where I wanted to make some point . . . but now I forget. It was all washed aside by an Oreo dream of crunchy, chocolatey sweet creamed forgiveness, and I would need to remember to buy some milk. A quart of milk; little kitty could drink what I wouldn't have. I have this little cat. He showed up one day at the back windowsill. I call him Bob. Bob the Cat. He's emotionally disturbed and likes milk and chicken best.

I nearly drained my beer in one wretched gulp. I know I don't have a job anymore, and I know everything seems so fucked up and I have no future. But that's okay. I got me here my last paycheck, you know. Two hundred some odd dollars. And I have a splendid bag of bagels. And some nice cream sodas and smoked salmon. And four pints of beer will do me just fine, thank you.

Then I thought about Her. The girl I no longer had. The girl I wanted. The girl I needed. I thought about Rachel. I could smell her right then. In the darkness at the back of the bar, as I looked out the door to the blinding light of bright summer midday, I could smell her once again. I inhaled deeply, distantly, the odor and warmth rising up off the crook of her neck as she lay gently sleeping in the bed. Our bed. Now just my bed and my bed alone.

I wanted to call her up. Call and hear her voice, to tell her, not that I had any words formulated, any message thus conceived. It's just that I thought, remembered really, and, well, I don't know, I found myself standing before the pay phone. Dropping the quarter into the slot, I dialed the number I still knew like my own. The gravity in The Yukon right then was simply stifling and yet . . .

"Hi, you've reached Rachel. I'm not home right now, but if you leave a message I'll get right back to you." I paused for a moment and then gently hung up the phone.

Her voice. That stupid-assed message. I swelled to overflowing. My eyes. My throat. I could barely breathe. It was too close to bear. I could see her. In my mind's eye I could see her and this mind Minolta never imagined. I saw Rachel in all her prettiest moments. When she'd be so sweet on me. The road trip we took. That time we had the crab.

I knew it was a fake. She wasn't The One, but now that she was gone, I loved her *so* much. I *knew* it was a farce, but I couldn't help but miss her badly. I couldn't help but feel empty and lost. I couldn't help but feel the pain. Gimme my pain! I want my pain, please!

I walked back to my empty seat and half-gone pint. I looked about the bar as though everyone was now in on my plight. Oh, Christ. Sweet Limpin' Christ!

I drained my glass and headed out the door like Ebenezer Scrooge, fully expecting a harsh and bitter wind and snowdrifts on the streets, but it was warm and there was not a cloud in the sky nor a wisp of fog.

At least I had my place. Good old Cedar Manor. And good old Mrs. Park. She's the Korean lady in B. I remembered after my first night, in the warm arms of then-sweet Rachel (before she suddenly and forever transformed into evil bitch–temptress Rachel), I found on my doorstep the next morning a big bowl of rice with a fishtail fried on top and tiny shaved green onions and ginger. Later that day Mrs. Park introduced herself and gave me a basket of plums and asked if I liked spring rolls, too.

But I didn't want spring rolls. I wanted Love and I thought about how great it would be when the day would come that I might have my girl by my side and the money to sport her a grand meal at Chez Panisse and we'd walk the five short blocks back to the beautifully crumbling Cedar Manor and step inside and slip under the cool sheets and fuck everybody else! I'll just stay here at the Cedar Manor in beautiful Berkeley Town with my someday-to-be-found Love and under the now-warmed animal lair blankets I'd melt into her arms, fall pleasant victim to her embrace, and watch the world collapse before our very love.

Brady

I awoke sometime around dusk to a pounding on my door. Kitty was curled up at the foot of the bed sleeping soundly. A bloodred light filtered in through the thin curtains of my bedroom window that faces the lush and overgrown backyard. My head ached from the morning's excitement and I was somewhat disoriented with . . . with everything.

Then it all came back to me. Oh, yeah, I'm the skinny, unemployed motherfucker with no woman and very little future. Cool. You see, a number of opportunities still lay at my disposal. I had the exciting prospect of next Monday's visit to the Employment Development Department and there was always good old Gramma to call for a small cash influx. That afternoon I felt not unlike an emerging Third World nation. Sure, things are fucked up right now, but with a bit of foreign aid, who knows what I might be capable of? My worth lay in my great potential and, really, it had always been such. The problem being that as I approached the ripe old age of thirty, the word "potential" always seems to want to be preceded by the word "wasted."

With my groggy head and disheveled reality close in tow, I dragged myself to the door. It was Brady, my new next-door neighbor pal.

Andy Brady had recently moved into the Cedar Manor from his cherished Texas, though he looked no different than your typical California freak. He was all tattoos and backward baseball caps that said "Lone Star Feed." He had piercings and rings of silver and skulls, copper bracelets, woven Indian wristbands, shredded Ts that either hawked some beat old diner down some dusty Texas road or some small-time speed metal band that played in some beat old bar down the same dusty road. And he had these eyes the color of the big summer sky from whence he came.

He grew up in this small town I'd once been through lost in the endless-in-all-directions heartland of West Central Texas. Kinda flat land, harsh and dry. The bushes all look sharp and gnarled and loaded with stickers and thorns. The barrenness of this near-desert land sliced here and thereabouts by a creek or river that disappears into the distance, leaving in its wake a trail of lush willows and dogwoods.

San Angelo was the town. Still is. Rachel and I passed through on our way back from our one great road trip. The trip to New Orleans to eat gumbo and étouffée. Café au lait and three hot powdered beignets at Café du Mond. The donuts and coffee seemed to bring the humidity out even more, a thick and clammy caress of Deep South green moisture.

I clearly remember the day Brady moved in. Somehow, by some minor miracle, the undersized yet hostile Pakistani, Satinder, had finally moved out of Cedar

Manor. Satinder—Mrs. Park called him The Viper—possessed a rodential glare, a sour disposition, and a squealing miniature pig that he used to carry about under his arm as he smarmily gathered his morning paper from the stoop.

It was the middle of the week. The Viper had moved on, though the pig's fate remained a mystery. The normally squealing pig had gone silent some ten days earlier and Satinder *had*, while peering out his window, been sucking on the last bits of meat hanging off a rather delicate chop on his last weekend at the Manor. But pig and Pakistani were now gone, and this made me happy.

I was inside my cottage, wondering why I was not yet rich and famous, when I heard a strange loud voice yelling something about "shit" and "fuckin'" and "dude." I peered out my window and saw two guys struggling with a ratty, fuchsia sofa. One guy was in a stocking cap and goatee and the other in a rumpled cowboy hat and goatee of his own. The second guy had on a pair of wraparound shades, and it was Brady.

It was like when a new kid moved in on the block. You're hoping it'll be somebody cool. Somebody like you, not somebody old and boring. Though I must admit this time around my mind spun with fantasies unparalleled for a dreamy cutie to move in all short skirts and tight pants. Why, I even had Christy Turlington moving into Cottage D, trying to "get away from it all."

After a grueling $50,000 day of modeling, Christy would walk up the steps to the Manor, the two of us exchanging furtive glances. After some time, I would introduce myself with this great opening line (I'm not sure of the line exactly; it remained a rough spot in my fantasy, so I moved on), and Christy would smile, her full lips drawing back across her perfect teeth, her endless feline eyes looking through me and then shyly downward. "Hi," she'd say as sweet as can be, and it was Love.

Actually, it was this drawling, homophobic, Ministry-lovin', beer-, tequila-, Jack-, and Turkey-swillin' fuckin' "pardner" fresh off the hardscrabble nothingness of West Central Texas: Andy Brady.

I opened the door and let him in. "What's up?"

"Oh, dude. What a fuckin' day." Brady shook his head. "I need a bong load or a beer or somethin'."

"Grab a beer outta the fridge," I offered.

Brady popped open a beer and settled into my lone frayed easy chair, sinking into its soft, ratty depths. He took a long swig and pushed the green and white paper hat back on his head. He was still in his uniform from the Chicken Shack where he worked. Brady liked to walk home in the uniform, his reasoning being that if you could walk the streets in that ridiculous garb, then the job itself became, somehow, less humiliating.

"Tough day at the fry vat?" I asked.

"That ain't even the half of it, dude."

"Yeah, well, it can't be as bad as my day. Since we got back from the airport, what, less than twenty-four hours ago? You won't believe this. I got fired *and,* AND Rachel and I broke up." I leaned back, sure of the trump of my tragedy.

"Huh? Yeah, well, check this out, dude. Homo tried to pick up on me again."

I just shook my head. Brady was something of a homophobe. It probably didn't help that the first time we went to San Francisco we ended up in the Castro and, I don't know, Brady kinda freaked. He was fresh off the range in his cowboy duds and he'd only *read* about gay communities, about their *possible* existence, and now he's in the thick of it dressed up like a cowboy and guys are hitting on him because Brady looks like maybe he's doing some sort of Village People thing.

Within five minutes, we were back in a cab heading to the relatively safe shores of North Beach, Brady ranting some fire and brimstone diatribe about the unnaturalness of homosexuality.

"It ain't right, dude," he said, shaking his head. "It just . . . ain't . . . right. I mean, they's wantin' to belly on up to the starfish?!"

"The what?!"

"You know." Brady furrowed his brow and performed some sort of circular hip motion that I took to mean homosexual anal man love. "I mean Keerist! They're right on out there with it."

"Relax."

"Djou see that one guy? In the shiny wet plastic gear with half his top torn off and a damn peg goin' through the boy's tit? What the fuck is that?"

"They ain't bothering anybody."

"Hell they ain't. Botherin' the shit outta me. I wanna see some guy in leather chaps I coulda just stayed in San Angelo and you can bet they wouldn'ta had their asses hangin' outta them, neither."

After that night, Brady became convinced that gays, like some Satanic cult, were out to get him. Brady was under siege. There was a twenty-four-hour threat to his flank. Basically, his ass was under attack and because of this alleged attempted takeover of his sexuality, this threat to his homelands, he carried with him a Cold War paranoia that convinced him that if he wasn't ever-vigilant, BANG! His ramparts could be rendered, his breeches breached, his starfish threatened.

"Did I get through, Brady?" I said. "Did you not hear? Buddy! Job: cashed. Girlfriend: history. Everything's all fucked up, man!"

"Yeah, well, listen to this," Brady started right in. "So today, I'm walkin' home from work, right? Goin' through campus, checkin' out all the pretties, scopin' the bulletin board, ya know? I'm sittin' a spell on this bench when this guy comes up, okay? Now, get this, if you will . . . in a wheelchair!

"He wheels right on up and starts in on starin' at me. It's so obvious. Plain as day. So after about two seconds I'm, 'What, dude?' and he's, 'What are you doing?' and I'm, 'Chillin',' and he's, 'What?' and I repeat, 'Chillin', buddy,' and he's, 'Huh?'

"Now, what am I, some fuckin' thesaurus? Chillin', restin', relaxin'. So anyways, he just hoists himself outta the chair and sits his ass right next to me. And I . . . mean . . . right . . . next." Brady karate chopped against his hip.

"It's those earrings," I said.

"It ain't the earrings, dude." Brady had a stud in his left ear and a small loop in the right. Back in San Angelo, where he'd been pierced, he wasn't sure if it was: left ear I'm cool, right ear I'm gay, or the other way around. So, to play it safe, he did 'em both.

"So now he's sitting right next to me," Brady continued, "and we start to talkin', and he tells me he's studying law, and I tell him I thought lawyers were kinda sleazy, ya know? So, now, get this, he's all 'You don't like sleazy? What's wrong with sleazy?' And, dude, he's got these crazy fuckin' eyebrows. Like that motherfucker in *Dune*. These fuckin' gigantic eyebrows are flyin' offa his head! They're goddamned wrigglin', dude! Every time he says 'sleazy' they're wagglin' and shit!"

Brady shook his head at the thought and took a drink off his beer. "So, it was 'Later, dude,' after that.

'I got an appointment, buddy. Sorry, Mr. Dune-eyebrowed, wheelchaired, sleazy-lovin' freak!' Damn."

I sat there, staring into space, more stunned by my day's developments than Brady's latest anal fears.

"Now, what were ya sayin'? You got fired?" Brady asked.

I nodded.

"Fuck, dude," he said.

"Want a bagel?" I asked.

"Nah, I ain't hungry."

"Some smoked salmon?"

"Nah, I ate a buncha chicken at work today."

"How 'bout a cream soda?"

"Nah, beer's cool. Your woman left ya, too?"

"Well . . ."

"On the same damned day?" he asked.

"Ah, I was getting sick of her shit, anyway."

"That's fucked up, dude."

"Yeah. Fuck her!"

"Hmmph. That's rough. What do ya think . . . ? Ah, never mind."

"What?" I asked.

"Forget it."

"What?!"

"Well . . . Nah, forget it."

"What, damn it!"

Brady stroked his goatee nervously. "Wouldja mind if I fucked her?"

"Get the fuck outta here."

"What? Is that so wrong?"

Gramma Was an Anti-Semite

It was the afternoon before Brady and I were to head into San Francisco for adventures beyond belief. I'd spent the morning alternating between violent torture scenarios involving my old boss, Shorter, and steamy reunion scenes concerning Rachel.

I've spent more time on the Rachel affair than I care to admit. I have it worked out to the tiniest detail: What she's wearing (usually something she can quickly shimmy out of or hoist up because, of the nineteen different situations I've concocted, *every* one of them ends with me fucking the shit out of her), how long it takes for her to break down in tears (usually not real long), her position (typically kneeling; as I see it, the best begging takes place on your knees, and I'm not even Catholic), the degree of my aloofness (normally inversely proportional to my actual desperation), and the various reasons why I *might not* be able to take her back (Christy Turlington's coming over any minute; I'm embarking tomorrow on my whirlwind rock star/spoken word world tour; my new weight lifting program has resulted in a gig as a Chippendales dancer, whatever).

By six o'clock, I'd pretty much mined this vein of insanity and still had an hour or so to kill before Brady got off work. I figured I should do *something* constructive, so I decided to call up Gramma and hope that she'd offer to send me some money.

Gramma liked to show me her love in the form of money orders of between fifty and seventy-five dollars, and seeing as I was out of work, I figured now would be a perfect time to allow Gramma to express these strong feelings.

Now, Gramma was an anti-Semite, but since I wasn't Jewish, the anti-Semitism didn't really affect me directly and, in fact, I was her favorite grandchild.

Gramma, like many good anti-Semites, came from Germany, and she wore gingham or floral print dresses with a bib apron, and her hair was always tied into two long gray braids. She looked a lot like Heidi if Heidi were about a hundred years old. Yet, strangely enough, despite the unnerving resemblance, our family in general and Gramma in particular *hated* Heidi and would have nothing to do with either her or her story, much to the dismay of Ole Sis, who secretly worshiped the smiling Swiss milkmaid.

I took a long, warm drink from my caffe latte doppio alto low-fat caffeinated beverage to ready myself and dialed Gramma up.

Gramma picked up after twenty rings and said, "Hello" in her what's-wrong voice that she used all the time.

S: Gramma?

G: Hello? Hello?

S: Gramma, it's me, Stevie.

47

G: Who?

S: Stevie.

Gramma's hearing was shot to hell, yet she refused to wear either her hearing aid *or* her dentures. To top it off, she was cranking the stereo. It was Wagner again.

S: Gramma! It's Steve!

G: Stevie? Is that you?

S: Yeah, it's me, Gramma.

G: Is something wrong? I can hardly hear you.

S: Everything's fine. Turn down the music.

G: I can't hear you. What's wrong? Gott im Himmel!

S: Nothing's wrong. Just turn down the music.

G: Ach, Gott! Gott im Himmel!

S: Gramma! Turn . . . Down . . . THE RADIO!

Now there was silence on the other end of the line. Just Wagner banging in the background and then nothing.

S: Gramma?

Now *I* was worried. She lived alone and Dear Old Dad kept threatening to honor her golden years by putting her in a home if she fell down anymore.

G: Stevie?

S: Gramma?

G: There, that's better. I turned off my music.

S: That's good. How you feeling today?

G: Oh, zo-zo. My artur-r-r-ritus, you know.

S: You got your bandages on?

G: Acch, yes. Thank you. And my Ben-Gay. You're such a good boy, Stevie.

Whenever she got going on the arthritis and the Ben-Gay, Gramma sounded like some Gestapo interrogator in a black leather coat. "Ve know you haff ze Ben-Gay." I could almost smell the stuff over the phone. The little apartment she lived in was practically coated in Ben-Gay and Raid. She loved the stuff. That and Ace bandages. After she slathered herself in a family-size tube of Ben-Gay, Gramma'd wrap any part of her that still moved with Ace bandages and G was good to go. She always wanted to use them on me when I was little. I tried to explain that little kids can't wear Ben-Gay and Ace bandages. That it just wasn't done. That I was already receiving sufficient beatings on the playground and didn't need to encourage the bullies further, but she was hard to tell shit to. In the end she'd defend herself with the irrefutable, "Don't tell me. I had to survive Hitler." There was no arguing that.

G: How is school going?

S: Uh, I graduated four years ago, remember, Gramma?

G: Ach du Leiber!

S: I was working at that bagel shop?

G: Gott im Himmel, not the Judens?!

S: It's just a bagel shop, Gramma. It's not like a synagogue.

G: You're going to a synagogue? AACCH!

S: Gramma . . .

G: Get a nice job, Stevie.

S: All right, Gramma.

G: Do that fur seine Grossmutti.

S: All right, I will.

G: How's that girl? She was so nice.

Gramma lived under the misconception that I was still going out with the girl I took to the high school prom. Never mind the near ten years gone by and the fact I now lived 600 miles away.

S: Um, well . . .

G: Does she love you?

S: Well, we're not going out anymore. Remember . . . ?

G: ACCHH, GOTT!!

Now Gramma was wailing. It wasn't like she would cry. Gramma never cried, but she could wail. Gramma would throw back her head, the long gray braids flying, roll her eyes, and emit a howl that made you think the entire world was falling apart that very moment.

G: Stevie, you've *got* to settle down! Like your sister.

S: Yeah, I know.

G: Get yourself a nice girl.

S: Sure.

This was gonna be harder than I imagined. Once she gets started on the Girlfriend Thing it's trouble. (I can't even bring up the *new* girlfriend who just dumped me. There's no hope getting Gramma up to speed on this!)

50

Gramma then launched into a fairy tale version of my sister's wonderful life: The devoted husband (yeah, Gramma, he's a mailman. He'll be killing coworkers any second now); the suburban house with the white picket fence (it's in the goddamned desert, dude!); the kids on the way (Gramma, don't you see? We *must* stop Dad's diabolical seed *this* generation?). It was no use arguing. It would be the same if I told her I smoked pot. Her head would just explode and then what? I was stuck. I decided to go for the preemptive strike.

S: I got fired from my job.

G: What?

S: I got fired the other day . . . but the boss, well, it was mostly his fault.

G: You quit your job?

S: Well, yeah. Sort of . . . Yeah.

G: Dank Gott im Himmel. You should never have worked for the Judens.

S: Gramma, the guy's name was Shorter.

G: Do you need some money, Stevie?

Ja Wohl!

High Desert Biker
Meth Lab

Billy Billingsgate carefully peered out the tiny, grimy window of The Shop after letting us inside. "Anybody follow you guys in here?"

"Nobody, Billy. It's just us," I said.

"Hmmm," he said skeptically as he latched the two dead bolts, rolled the oil drum in front of the door, and again peeked out the window. "How you so sure?"

"Who's gonna be followin' us, Billy?" Brady asked and cracked open a forty of O.E.

"Oh, you think I'm gonna tell you who's followin' me? You think I'm fuckin' stupid?"

"Have a beer, man," I said. "We brought a couple of forties for you."

"Don't mind if I do." Billy grabbed the bottle, cracked off the top, took a long slug, and then returned to his work deep under the hood of his gorgeous sapphire blue '67 Pontiac GTO.

"Hand me that fuckin' five-eighths-inch socket, will ya?" he asked, his empty hand appearing from under the hood. Brady plopped the socket into Billy's hand, which disappeared back under the hood. A couple of ratchet clicks and Billy pulled his head out, looked about The Shop suspiciously, and then said, accusatorially, "Japs could never make shit like this fuckin' baby. This is American motherfuckin' steel, boys! Detroit SHIT!" And with that, he disappeared back into the engine compartment.

Billy was the time-warped ex-hippie biker who lived in Cottage E. He was probably nearing fifty, but because he was time-warped, you couldn't really tell how old he was. He was just Billy the Biker Dude and he always would be.

Billy claimed to be the last Hell's Angel in all of Berkeley. Why, he even had himself a denim jacket with the sleeves cut off that said "Oakland Chapter" on the back. And he had himself a bandanna hat he wore over his red hair that fell in thick curls to his narrow shoulders. And he had himself a scraggly beard that covered his sunken, acne-scarred cheeks. And he had himself some big old black boots with straps on them. And he had himself a ratty T-shirt that said "Harley-Davidson" or "Black Sabbath."

And Billy had himself The Shop, where he held court and tore apart and put back together internal combustion machines, entertaining the boys with tales from his salad days when he was ripe and randy and rough and ready and haulin' up and down the beautiful State of California.

The Shop was cluttered with all sorts of ancient shit: concert posters from the sixties, Led Zeppelin ticket stubs, blacklight artwork, vintage bongs and broken down hookahs, thirty-year-old albums, abalone shell ashtrays, a Marantz receiver and Dual turntable. He had a battered guitar he claimed was once owned by Richie Blackmore, an Angus Young pool cue, and a Tony Iommi fake ring finger. Shit like that. Shit you really couldn't be sure of, but with Billy . . . who knows?

Billy's Shop was what I imagined a high desert biker meth lab might look like. It was like a wrecky Hard Rock Cafe without the food 'cause Billy rarely ate, what with the pounds of crystal he was constantly jamming up his nose. In fact, that was one of the reasons we came over in the first place. To see if Billy wouldn't set us up for a good long night. For the price of a six-pack or a pepperoni pizza, Billy'd let you into the inner sanctum of The Shop and, who knows, maybe let you have a taste of his wares.

He'd be workin' on the car or on his Harley, we'd hand him tools, all of us takin' swigs offa beers or a bottle of Jack, smokin' cigs or buds, and then maybe Billy'd offer you a little line or a fat dot of crystal. That shit would hit you hard in the bridge of the nose, practically knock you off your feet, but then you'd be off and goin' and that's what we were after.

"Hey, Billy," Brady said. "Reeves and I are goin' into The City tonight. Wanna come?"

Billy stuck his head out from under the hood. "Oh, yeah. Right, man. Like I'm gonna go into the fuckin' CITY!"

"Just askin'," Brady said.

"Well, nice try, cowboy. Those fuckin' Hunters Point boys I'm sure would like to get a piece a ol' Billy. They been waitin' years to get a piece a ol' Billy. Shit." Billy took another long drink off his malt liquor and disappeared back under the hood.

Billy wasn't real big on ever leaving his cottage or The Shop. I'm not sure how he got any food besides the pizza and beer we would bring over. He got out about as often as Miss Havisham and, as a result, was a rather pale and paranoid fellow. Billy pulled his head out from under the hood again and asked Brady, "You workin' for those boys?"

"Huh?" Brady asked.

"You workin' for those boys?"

"What . . ."

"Trying to trick ol' Billy?"

"What boys?" Brady asked.

"Hmmm, you better not be, Tex, or they'll be takin' you back to Mama in a body bag." Billy shot Brady his evil eye for added effect and disappeared under the hood.

Billy had this left eye. This jickity-jacked left eye. It was vaguely clouded and the pupil misshapen as though a hole had been pricked in the bottom and the black had run out, staining the lower half of his pale gray iris.

This fucked-up eye required two things of all visitors to The Shop. First off, don't be fuckin' lookin' at it. He was a mite sensitive about that eye. Billy had distilled his insecurities about his looks—his lanky frame, his sallow complexion, his bad skin, and ratty beard—down to the misshapen eye. Anyone caught looking at it got one warning, and if one wasn't enough, well, you better view fisticuffs with the same sporting relish that Billy claimed.

The second thing about the eye was that Billy really couldn't see very well out of it. He had a rather massive blind spot to his left. Combined with the crystal paranoic world in which he resided, this made approaching Billy from that side a somewhat dangerous prospect. The one time that I did (how was I to know you couldn't approach the guy from an entire side? Who could guess that?) Billy flinched away from me as though I might cuff him one up side the head and then took a wild roundhouse punch at me. He missed me by a whisker because, if nothing else, I have very quick reflexes. I can pluck a falling beer bottle out of midair, you know.

"Looga this fuckin' piece a shit, will ya?" Billy stood up from the engine compartment of the GTO and held up a worn spark plug for us to examine. "You see this little motherfucker?"

"It's called a spark plug," Brady answered smartly.

"Oooh," Billy cringed in mock fear and took a big hit off his forty and then one off his Marlboro 100. "Tex sure knows his cars."

"Don't call me Tex, okay?" Brady tried to be nice.

Billy tossed the plug in a high arc and Brady snatched it. "Now, the funny thing is," Billy continued, "the *funny* thing . . . is we all seen a fuckin' spark plug. I bet even Reeves here could ID one for us, but I bet none of you fuckers ever seen a plug with two points. Have you?"

"I seen a snake with two heads once," Brady offered.

"*I'm* talkin' spark plugs here." Billy turned to me. "I don't recall any bullshit Alice in Wonderland crap about reptiles."

"Spark plugs." I nodded.

"Thank you. So . . ." Billy paused and looked hard at Brady with his jacked eye. "I could just kick your fuckin' ass in about two minutes. You do know that, don't you . . . Tex?"

"Don't be callin' me Tex," Brady said.

"Oh, is that so . . . ?"

"Come on, Billy," I said, "what about the plug?"

"Well." Billy smiled and took another long tug off his forty. "I am glad you asked."

Billy had a bit of an attention disorder. His mind could latch on to anything at any moment: I'm drinkin' a beer, I'm fixin' the car, that reminds me about spark plugs, whoops now I'm pissed off and want to kick your ass. His train of thought worked like that, and the train invariably ended up at the Kick-Your-Ass Station.

"Now, they came up with the fuckin' twin spark plug years ago, man," Billy continued. "It was a break-through, man. A fuckin' BREAKTHROUGH! But we never seen one, and why the fuck is that?

". . . WELL!?" Billy actually screamed.

Brady and I shrugged.

"Gas mileage, boys. Can't be improving gas mile-age."

"Why wouldn't somebody just make 'em and get rich selling the things?" I boldly offered, hoping this wouldn't elicit Billy's usual generous offer of a good beating.

"Nobody'd distribute the fuckers, College Boy. Didn't think of that, didja?" Billy was so pleased, he simply had to drain the rest of his malt liquor. "Nope, couldn't sell 'em and even if you tried, well, Shell, Chevron, they got whole R & D teams workin' twenty-four/seven pullin' the wool over everybody's fuckin' eyes, makin' 'em think they need fancier shit that ain't worth a damn."

I'm not sure why, but I always liked it over at Billy's. Sure, he was racist and sexist and vulgar and crude and often physically threatening, but he kinda grew on you after a while. Spinning his tales of deviltry and conspiracy. But then our relationship was vastly simplified by the fact that I utterly and completely accepted as the Gospel Truth that Billy could kick my fuckin' ass at any time and under any condition. I didn't necessarily believe it, but the first time I met him, looked into that

57

cloudy gray eye of his, and Billy barked out, "What's your name?" like it was a threat, I just shot him one of those subconscious primal looks of deferment, like a dog that creeps up to a bigger, tougher one, sidlin' up sideways, its tail waggin', and rolls over on its back to reveal its soft, white underbelly as the ultimate sign of submission. Yeah, I shot him one of those and we got along just fine after that.

Brady, on the other hand, was not so lucky. First off, he was from Texas, which for some reason got Billy *extra* riled. It seems that for some people, the world just isn't big enough for both Texas *and* California. On top of that, Brady never shot Billy that look of deferment that Billy sought. The look that crowned Billy "King of the Shop" and Billy *knew,* he could smell it like an animal, see it in Brady's eyes, that Brady entertained the notion that maybe he could take Billy if it came down to it.

So their relationship was marred by having to deal with this unresolved issue a lot. After the right number of beers, or when it got late enough, or if Billy was crashin' from the meth, maybe it was just from breathing the fumes from all the solvents Billy had layin' around The Shop, I don't know, but sooner or later, Billy and Brady'd be starin' each other down like two stupid moose in a terrible rut. Luckily, it was still early and things were fairly calm.

"I got fired this week," I told Billy.

"Huh? You what?" Billy had just done a fat dot and was holding his nose. He offered me the mirror. "You want some?"

"Sure." I did a couple of small dots. "Jesus! That shit burns!"

"Damn straight, Captain," Billy said. "Now, what the fuck did you just SAY!?"

I handed the mirror to Brady. "I said I got fired from my job."

"Ah, shit!" Billy took it real personal for a second and then said, "Well, fuck that fuckin' JOB! Where were you workin', anyway? Candy factory?"

"Candy factory?! You're thinkin' of Jeffrey Dahmer. I was at the BagelWorks."

"Ahh," he waved his hand and made a sour face. "Fuck them. What the fuck do you need a job like that for, anyway? You're fuckin' College Boy!"

"I need money."

The Shop fell silent. Everyone looked down at the floor, nodding, paying their private respects to Money. Money, there was no denying. It was the only complete truth anyone had come up with since Descartes. I think, therefore I am . . . now gimme some bank! Anything beyond that was pure speculation.

Brady broke the silence as he cracked open his second forty and informed Billy, "Homo tried to pick up on me again . . ."

Night and the City

My crappy car (which usually ran so badly that from here on out I'm just gonna call it The Car so the manufacturer doesn't get all bent out of shape at me telling everybody how crappy the cars they make really are) started right up. I let it warm up as Brady finished his second forty. I'd already shattered my lifetime record for most bowel movements in a twelve-hour period and now sat there wondering if Billy's crystal wasn't causing a minor heart attack. My chest was pounding and I was breathing in short gasps like some sexually aroused gerbil.

I turned on the radio and was thankfully swept away on the music. For once a good song was on. Something with hard chords and balls, something meaty and thumping with a deep, primitive jungle beat, so I cranked it up and now I was rollin'. Fuck everything else! We gots places to go tonight and adventures to be had, I tell you, and I can hardly convey to you the serious good omen that the car starting and the radio cloaked in fine tunes meant to me right then. Brady began to gently nod his head to the beat and I tentatively hit the gas to see if the car might also move forward.

"Baby, this car wants to move. Yeah!" Brady yelled as we pulled out. Usually hitting the accelerator was the car's cue to stall. Any attempt at forward movement had to be coaxed and cajoled out of the car. While somewhat rational and not given to the party line astrological New Age power-pointed positivistic philosophy of the day, I would still speak to my car in the morning. Complete lip-moving pleas aloud for it to fucking please start for once! But as I said, tonight the gods were on our side and the omens all aligned and off we went.

We were both smiling and joking and laughing as we blended onto the freeway and made our way to the Bay Bridge. The clear night sky, the good radio songs, the release of flying sixty miles an hour down an open road, it was Joy, I tell you!

We zipped up to the toll plaza all electrified in yellows and greens and reds. I saw the toll booth takers and thought, Oh, man what a world is that? And as I paid, I felt a pang of grief for the black woman in the tiny fume-filled booth, taking my money, the dollar bill I held out stiff in the night air. She took my money the way she took all the endless dollar bills from a full-shift procession of endless cars. The nameless faces, the faceless forms. My pain for her was real and up front, sitting there on the dashboard, when Brady said to me, "Here, dude, give this here to that pretty girl with the wild dreads takin' our dollars tonight."

I handed her the two airline bottles of gin that Brady had miraculously produced as he leaned over with a twinkle in his eyes and a long smile. "Evenin' sweetheart." Her face lit up as she slipped the bottles into her pocket and shot us a sweet look of unexpected joy. For tonight we *are* Joy, my friend.

On we sped to The City and now we were *really* flying. All was right with the world, and anything was possible. Just anything at all. It was all laid out before us: A big old world all stocked and lit up beyond compare, and who could say what might happen tonight, and right then I *knew* I dreamed dreams I dare not think.

As we climbed up the bridge, the night was alive and aglow. The moon just past full sat above the Oakland Hills and the stars were out but invisible for all the light. But they were up there, nonetheless. You just knew.

It was clear as we hit Treasure Island, but as we came out of the tunnel, at the first big sight of wondrous San Francisco, you could see the fog, the fog that was never to leave me that summer, its thick fingers creeping east above the waters of the bay. Thin wisps of it floating high as you looked up and saw Coit Tower, all the skyscrapers in their monumental Manhattan madness, the Embarcadero, the Ferry Building, and in big lights and bright: Port of San Francisco. That makes it official. Let the games begin!

Everything yelled to us, screamed with Life as we laughed and raced down the Bay Bridge all lit up, the moon fat and shimmering, the distant lights twinkling off Marin and Alameda. Like us, all light was drawn into San Francisco. It was sucked in and touched down with the Transamerica building, slipped up the alleyways of crazy Chinatown and the sizzling Mission, the Heights, the Haight, and tawdry, sad, yet godlike North Beach. All was drawn into The City for an instant and then instantaneously reflected back into the night more alive and wondrous than it might otherwise ever have been.

"Suck it up, dude!" Brady was hooting as he smoked a cigarette. Brady filled me with an excitement. He'd come to town like a wide-eyed kid, like a tourist, no disrespect, but he could look at the Golden Gate Bridge in sincere awe and I'd think, yeah, I seen it a million times before, but Brady could get you to see it all over again. See it with the excitement of the new-comer, with the novelty and wonder of First Time. "Damn! I wish we was in a convertible right now. Boy, then . . ." and his face flushed with that seductive thought.

And suck it up I did as the bridge carried us over the dark waters of the bay. The water sat silent, pos-sessed somehow of a greater mass. It was a liquid black hole. During the day, a beautiful day, all could be dashed with but one glance at the choppy gray waters of the bay. The Sun. The Blue Sky. The fresh breeze and summer on the way, but a single look at the terrific roiling waters of the San Francisco Bay and all could crumble, so Medusa-like were its powers. But this night the inky waters, while never entirely relinquishing their malevolence, provided only our triumph as the bridge carried us up and over and into The City. Into China-town for a bite to eat, to Specks for a quick drink, we'll pay our respects to City Lights and Kerouac Lane and then let the Sirens of the Night take us where they may, by god!

We were at our first bar and, well, a bar, my friend, can be something stumbled into as though out of des-tiny's dream, or it can be searched high and low upon the whispered rumor of the street (usually all fucked up) until one night you step into a particular establishment and Bam! you know you have at last arrived. It has the special atmosphere this traveler requires. An ambience much needed. Now, I could tell you about Andy Boy's or El Rio, the Swede's or The Congo, but the name doesn't matter much, and by the time word reaches you, the party's left, and it's not about *where* really. It's about *you*. Where are *you* tonight?

At this first bar, Brady and I lucked into a table off to the side, and we started in on chatting up some girls. Well, Brady mostly. He was champing for action while I was chillin'. I just sat back and looked over the two girls. The anorexic one in the big corduroy hat seemed to be the one Brady telepathically bestowed upon me, while he leaned into the other one. The big blonde. Why, this girl must have been six foot and curvy, too. But as I said, I wasn't getting caught up, living and dying over these girls' attention. I was just sipping my beer. The evening was just begun and I was just along for the ride.

That night I was Waiting. Clouds in the Heavens. The superior man eats, drinks, and is joyous and of good cheer. No resistance, nothing forced. The chips and the evening could fall where they may and by this complete giving of myself, my relinquishing of my Free Will to the night, I would realize the most of all. And already we were chatting up a couple girls, plugging into the electricity that seemed to hang in the very air we breathed.

Next it was the club down off the Mission where there was live music and we all wanted that. As the first band took the stage, Brady fast-downed the last third of a bottle of beer. He was now drinking at a heroic pace, fueled by Billy's crystal.

"Come on, dude," he said to me, "Ain't no fun way

out here on the sidelines. Fella's gotta get in the game to get any glory."

I finished my beer. It reminded me of summers at the beach in San Diego when I was a kid and it was decided now was the time to test the waters and enter the surf. I slipped my glasses into my pocket and followed Brady into the surging tide of the mosh pit.

The bass rumbled. The singer began a scream from deep within his crouched and coiled stance. The guitars began to chop and the crowd erupted in a hair-swinging, sweat-flying frenzy. We bounced and spun and flew about. Banging into each other in one of the few complete releases I'd ever known—besides, maybe, disappearance into a soft kiss. Bodies were cartwheeling about and flying from the stage, people were screaming, heads were nodding, eyes roamed the room, hands nervously gripped $3.50 bottles of beer, and smoke hung in the rafters as the room filled with an ecstatic release of energy, filled with an animal passion, a November rut with thundering bass line that throbbed to the core of our very existence. It was pure and blissful insanity. Inanity. A requited calamity which fully absorbed me.

After a break, we were leaning against the bar. The place was packed and loud and I wiped the sweat off my brow. As the night progressed, with each tick of the clock, each tip of his beer, Brady slipped further and further back to his old Texas self. His Texas blood boiled to the surface, and he became more and more that good old boy from San Angelo, ridin' horses and huntin' for deer with his uncle, who he used to tell tales about, some soggy old drunk, too. Brady told me all the stories. He told me *all* of them. The burning down of the Country Club, the sawing in half of the poodle (whether it was alive or dead at the time always remained gray and nebulous). Stories told in hushed tones or a sense of long-sitting regret. He told me these stories like I could make sense of them somehow, or that the simple telling of them might make his world fall into place.

And when he told these country boy stories of his country boy past, he would rail on and denigrate this past, reject his heritage, paint himself in the wronged light of an exile from his clan, an expatriate from what none of us knew but all of us understood. But, really, it *was* his past that made him, that gave him his identity, his power, it was when he seemed most real and potent. And I envied him for having a past. A tribe. An identity that I would never know. Andy Brady from San Angelo, Texas.

"So how'd you come to Berkeley, anyway?" I asked.

"I don't know. It's radical, dude. I mean, come on!"

"Radical? Like you were gonna join a march or something?"

"Fuck you, dude! You ain't grown up in some bunk-assed town like I'd been. So what the fuck do you know?"

"All right, all right. I was just wondering. Keep your fucking pants on."

"Well, why the fuck'djou move up here? What's wrong with San Diego?"

As he asked me this question, I realized I viewed my family as a crime committed in some past life. That I now attempted to operate under the guise of another. I was the fuckin' Fugitive!

"I don't know, man," I said. "San Diego was fucking killing me. Nice place to visit, though . . ."

"All right, that's cool." Brady waved me off.

"Now, then, tell me about Yosemite again. We gotta go there one of these days, you know."

"I'm fuckin' ready. Let's go."

"Well, all right, then. It's all good."

We headed down a few blocks to another club because the grass is always greener, the music always better, and the dreams of girls always greater. As we made our way through the pool room to where a band had just begun, a group of guys who looked like white Urkels got up and left, leaving us a table and seats front row, and the band was fucking ripping, I tell you! The bare-chested drummer rolled endless thunder. The bassist noodled along at a frantic pace. They had a guitarist and even a trumpet player, man! One lit up red, the other blue.

At one point, the guitarist broke out into a spoken word riff, snapping his fingers cooly, languidly, to the raw jazz beat in his vintage slacks and jacket, the trumpeter wailed long-haired modern in old wool pants. The whole band jammed away to heavens of their own invention, and the music swept the entire room up to godlike visions of our own devices. It was Beat, and I was there. How I wanted it to be the fifties again. Sudden death from the Russians our only fear.

After a bit, at the end of the first set, Brady went off to try and get in a game of pool, and I headed to the bar for another beer, DUI's be damned! I waited forever, for, you see, I have the warlock's ability to disappear completely as I lean against a bar, hoping to buy a drink. Buzzards circle overhead before the barkeep ever looks my way. Well, Clouds in the Heavens flowed with the bartender's neglect, I savored my quiet moment of waiting, when appeared at my side a slight wisp of a woman, a girl, really, waiting like myself, and we smiled and agreed the last band was good and I boldly said the words, the often poisonous words of "Buy you a beer?" Words that make 75 percent of all women recoil with a sneer or fear, maybe a polite "No thanks," but this girl blossomed at the offer, eager and miraculous.

"Awright." She smiled. She had bright red hair, a pointy chin, and thin lips, but her eyes were dreamy and anxious and I smiled back and swallowed hard once.

The band began again, and we stood at the back of the room, swaying to the music, tentative glances punctuated with sips off our bottles. There was a bit of body contact and some brushing of hands, if you know what I mean, and after a bit she leaned toward me and said, "Lemme buy you a beer, now."

We found a table off to the side, and during a break we chatted a bit. She was from up in Washington, went to school there, was here visiting some friends. I filled in some small bits of a bio of my own. It wasn't important. By then our universes had converged upon our index fingers as they locked and tugged and pulled away shyly, all the time our hands wrapped around our bottles of Anchor Steam.

As the lights went down and a new band took the stage, she released that bottle and slid her chair next to mine, our backs against the cool concrete wall, our faces in the hot club air, and suddenly we're in a soft kiss, she came out of nowhere, her slight frame pressing against mine.

And this girl could kiss, that thin-lipped redheaded lass from up Spokane way. A farm girl true as any, she would melt for a moment in my mouth and we'd hold each other in that moist, warm, vast instance, hanging onto each other's lips, our eager, rolling tongues pressing for more than our very souls and, I swear, I thought I could taste apples on the sweet breath of this redhead from Washington State.

After a good long bit, we'd break for air, kinda embarrassed for a moment with all the people milling about, looking away from each other, our eyes uncertain of the intimacy that our mouths craved. And I know her friend must be watching from somewhere and she's tripping on that, but I just laid eyes on this girl not twenty minutes ago, and I'm as thrilled as can be as I again lean into her and take her mouth, moist lips parted, our tongues again wrestling in an ever-heating clench. What great luck for Clouds in the Heavens as I lose myself in a kiss, her breathing picking up. I rub my hands slowly along her T-shirted rib cage. I do detect some grunts on her part and a groan of my own, now that you mention it.

The band stops, the lights come up, our universe is dashed as we break for air and laugh nervously.

"Dude, 'sup?" It's Brady, the last person I want to see right then. "Who's your little friend?"

"I gotta go," she just said? But wait! We both stood up. I'm holding her hand until she walks away from arm's length with a smile more enticing than Life itself, and before I realize what's happening, down the stairs she goes, and I follow downstairs and out the door and into the moist, foggy, San Francisco summer night. The fresh, cool air sizzling on the alcohol and lust warmth of my cheeks.

She was gone. I looked up and down the street and walked up to Seventeenth to make sure. The streets were loud and packed and lit up. Alive she was, old San Francisco. I don't care what anybody tells you, she's the finest city I could ever know, so let's love her up like the rangy ragged momma that she be. All-forgiving, all-comforting San Francisco.

I near rolled upon the sidewalk in happy laughter. The girl was gone, back to Spokane for all I knew, but I licked my still-tingling lips in the remembrance and felt alive and growing.

As we walked back to The Car, Brady and me, talking about sweet girls, our heads swimming with ale, I thought I could make out every water molecule suspended in the oncoming night's breeze. It was a big night's fog, and with each step toward dawn, the fog gained in substance. It lost any ethereal quality it possessed as thin wisps licking just above the pavement. This shit was like clouds, and you could feel the moistness in the top of your lungs if you breathed a little deeper.

There was a purity to it, same as wood ash from a fine log fire. Gray and pure. The fog blew in from across the vast Pacific. It was as innocent and perfect as I could imagine amid the crumbling concrete, my wrecked life, the dawn of the Third Millennium. That night, the fog washed it all away, and I was very happy walking with bold strides and a broad grin pasted across my face.

I dropped down upon my mattress. It had been a good night. We had marched up to the trough, as Brady had so beautifully and drunkenly put it, and sucked up on Life, and walked away satisfied, wiping our dripping mouths with the backs of our sleeves.

I looked out my bedroom window all silver in the light of the waning Scorpio moon, my room lit pearly and serene. I thought about the little redhead from up Washington way, all country girl, and I swear this sweetheart tasted of apples.

My head spun in a delightful delirium as magically,

miraculously, it all floated away. All the slights and the feuds, all the unfairness and the hurts. Rachel. Shorter. Evil Dad. It all became lighter than air and lifted away into the night sky.

I felt again the warm glow on my lips from the girl. I felt snug and whole in my room without her. I tried to smell her on my hands and as I slipped off to sleep, I imagined burying myself into her waiting throat.

Hello?!

The coughing man just will not stop. And that coat he's wearing, it's so shabby. It seems to be disintegrating while he sits and waits for his number to be called. How long has he been here? How long have *I* been here?

"Hrack! Hrack! Hrack!" his lungs rumble clottily. He holds a hand over his mouth in a last vestige of civility. The hand is cloaked in a tattered wool glove despite the fact that it's nearly July. He seems to have been transported here from Dickens's London.

As I sit in my plastic seat at the Employment Development Department, I have the disturbing realization that my world has forever changed. The drunken elation of seventy-two hours before has vanished in the face of this man's tuberculosis. The hard-wiring placed in my brain by Dear Old Dad has rendered me tense regarding my financial and sexual predicaments. My balances are coming up short. I'm in immediate need of fiscal advisors and couples counseling.

72

The simple sight of the dreary brick building (it's the only damn brick building left in town after the earthquake retrofits) and the people milling about in front, clutching paper bags hiding cans of early-morning malt liquor, was cause enough for alarm. Entry into the place is a signal that one's wonderful life isn't quite progressing as planned. My world has crumpled around me like a Yugo in a head-on.

"Number forty-three?" the woman with the thick glasses calls out.

I reach into my pocket for my number and when I don't find it, I go through a hot-collared search as though this tiny piece of paper holds some key to my future (which, technically, it does). When I at last locate it the news isn't good: I hold number fifty-one.

I get up to inquire, but the guard standing in the corner wearing sunglasses stares me down. He has a nightstick in his right hand and he passes the time slapping it into the palm of his left.

The coughing man's shaved head seems strangely different, as though the skin were stretched extra tight over his cranium. He's a bit short on skin, perhaps. And the skin he has seems almost translucent. I can nearly make out the skull beneath. Surely this can't be helping in his quest for employment.

The guard in the corner seems to particularly enjoy smacking his nightstick menacingly into the palm of his hand whenever I look his way. This is my first visit to the EDD. Maybe there's an unwritten rule: Don't Fucking Look at the Guard!

I begin to fill out my mountain of forms.

What was your last position?

Uh, unwitting assistant to one of Satan's minions? While *I* feel this to be an accurate description of my position at the BagelWorks, I have an idea this will not garner me the fistfuls of unemployment benefits I am after. I put down: Counter help at a Jewish bread products shop.

Why did you leave this position?

I really want the world to know that Shorter was the Devil's lackey and $6.50 an hour is not sufficient pay to burn for Eternity in Hell, but I know what they're looking for: laid off for lack of work (which is somewhat true; I did very little).

List all relevant job skills.

This part's gonna be tricky. I pretty much don't have any. I do fairly well when I watch *Jeopardy!* on TV, but that's probably not relevant. I can boil bagels and make change out of a cash register as well as identify and spread seventeen different cream cheese schmears. I once filled burlap sacks at a horseradish plant. I did a summer of soul-squashing door-to-door work for a nonprofit organization. I *do* have that college diploma and know quite a bit about Karl Marx. Let's see . . . I worked at a restaurant so I *am* able to cut and wash vegetables and bone out chicken breasts. I wonder if there's a great demand in the job market for garlic peelers or horseradish sack fillers who understand Marxist dialectics? Then I remember: commercial fisherman.

I had a job one summer on a swordfishing expedition back when I lived in San Diego. It was a small commercial boat and we'd fish for swordfish with harpoons like Moby-Dick. When we nailed one, it was my job to throw the lines and buoys overboard without wrapping anything around my ankles. Then we'd let the poor creature swim around until it got tired and we could hoist it on board and pound in its head with a baseball bat. I know it sounds brutal, but I'm assuming this was proper procedure. It was my only swordfishing expedition, so I have nothing to compare it to, but the captain and the engine guy seemed pretty cool. There was lots of beer and they sure fired up the spliffs every evening as the sun faded into the Pacific. It'd be warm and golden off Ana Capa, your face glowing from the heat of the day, a can of Bud in your hand, and the boat gently swaying in the summer ocean.

"Number forty-seven? . . . forty-seven?!"

I do believe the State of California is trying to wait me out. They figure with the damaged attention spans people have these days, no one will be able to sit here the required fifteen hours it takes to process a claim. Well, they don't know who they're dealing with here.

The man in front of me is now making sounds like a barking mastiff. I snap open my newspaper in front of my face as a sort of postapocalyptic shield against the amazing and unknown diseases I now imagine him to possess.

Forget him. On 8A of the *Chronicle* I strike gold! It's all laid out in black and white. They've got statistics, graphs, illustrations, everything. It seems the world is coming to an end, the scientists just can't settle on the exact date. But they have all the proof.

Seventy-five percent of all bird species in the next ten years? Cashed!

Virgin forests? Forget it.

Last 500 years? Game over for 85 percent of all large land mammals.

Frogs? Fuckin' history.

Plants are disappearing. Human population bomb's been exploding since the first Earth Day. Boiling of all water will be mandatory by the time I strap on my first pair of Depends. Wow! The planet is going downhill even faster than myself. Cool! I'm not alone. We're *all* doomed.

I carefully close the paper. There is no time to weep for the lowland gorilla because this man's cough has taken on dimensions that I feared from the beginning.

"Hruckh! Hruckh! Hraack!" he rattles phlegmatically from deep within his lungs.

"Whoochk! Whoochk! Whooeeeekk!" He seems to be making almost birdlike sounds and the entire room turns toward him with looks of concern, disbelief, and unmitigated hate. Uh-oh, here comes the guard.

"Number fifty-one? . . . fifty-one?!"

"Hello?!" the woman in the horn-rimmed cat-eyed glasses says for the thousandth time. She keeps saying it in this singsong question/shout that's really beginning to piss me off.

"Hello?! We're not talking about swordfishing, young man. Unh-unh," she simultaneously shakes her head and wags her pointed forefinger (which, incidently, is equipped with the longest, most raptor-curled fingernail I've ever seen; she clutches her pen like a burn victim) in an emphatic "No!"

"I was just sayin' . . ."

"I *asked* you about how you left your last job."

"Okay, well, I was in the boss's office, right? And I said, 'Lotta work to do' and dickweed says . . ."

"Wait wait wait wait wait wait wait. It says *here* your boss's name is Shorter."

"Um, yeah. That was his assistant. Mr. Weed. Richard Weed. Uh . . . but I don't think he works there anymore."

I'm not sure why, but things quickly went sour at Window E. By the time we agreed on my zip code, I was already belligerent, visions of returning with the Colt .45 and going out in a blaze of mailman glory flashing through my head. It's as though F. Lee Bailey was examining my claim ("Isn't it true, sir, that you have a drinking problem?").

I begin to get hot around the collar. The room almost begins to spin and I feel light-headed. I *need* this money. The mere thought of having to immediately find another lousy job fills me with a free-falling anguish.

"So, wait a minute, dude," Brady said. "Then the guard actually walked your ass outta the dang building?!"

We were sitting in Brady's living room. Empty beer bottles littered the place, and the smell of stale cigarettes and sour bong water filled the air. We were both sucking on juicy chicken bones from eight boxes of Chicken Shack Grampa's Original and Grampa's Extra Crispy that Brady'd brought back from work.

"Tain't stealin'," Brady assured me as though stealing would stop him, given the right circumstances. "They cain't sell it no more. Been in the danger zone too long."

"Danger zone?!" I held a drumstick gingerly by its knuckle.

"Yeah, you know, bacteria-infestin' temp'atures," Brady said nonchalantly, taking another thigh out of a box of Extra Crispy.

I looked at the drumstick for a second, as though I might be able to spot some microbes. Then I thought again. I thought about my day at the EDD, about the world coming to an end, about my own no-girl, no-job, no-money reality. I took a big succulent bite out of an O. G. leg and said, "But it's free."

"Damn straight, dude. Just keep a bottle of Pepto nearby . . . just in case. Now, what'd ya do to get that guard all riled up?"

"Nothing, man! It was right after I began yelling at

77

the woman, 'one hundred and four dollars a week? That's it!?' I don't know, I kept saying it over and over and over and the next thing I knew, the guard had me by the arm and led me to the door, saying something about them contacting me by mail. One hundred and four dollars a week can't be right. Can it?"

Brady shrugged. "So you don't have to go back?"

"I'm pretty sure he specifically said *not* to come back."

"That's cool. How long's it take till ya hear?"

"They call up Shorter at the 'Works and see if my story's straight, and then I get a check."

"Hope Shorter don't fuck with ya."

"Fuck with me?" I asked and decided to school Andy Brady on mailmen and their progeny.

"Your dad's a mailman?" Brady asked.

"Yeah. That's right."

"D'he have a uniform?"

"OF COURSE!" I screamed. "Whaddaya think? He had a fuckin' pith helmet."

"He had a pith helmet?"

"Yeah he did. And he had this shit you spray in dog's faces if they were giving you trouble."

"No shit."

"You know about mailmen, right?" I asked.

"Guys that deliver the mail?"

"Hmmph. They go off."

Brady took a long drag off his post–danger-zone chicken feast cigarette. "You mean killin' their own kind and such?"

"Exactly. D'ya ever hear of Patrick Sherrill?"

"Cain't say that I have."

"He was the King. He was the Manson of Mailmen. The Juan Corona of Carriers. Oh, there have been others. Plenty. But no one has ever come close to matching Crazy Pat. That's what his neighbors called him."

"What'd'e do?"

"Well, on August 20, 1986, part-time letter carrier Patrick Sherrill, he walks into the Edmonds, Oklahoma, branch of the U.S. Post Office. He'd been having a little trouble at work. Bosses ridin' him, customers hassling him, he was even written up the day before for doing shitty work, so he was pretty pissed off by now. He shows up that morning armed with two Colt .45s, just like the one I got, ya know? And a .22 revolver. He's got it all stashed in his mail bag. Ten minutes later, fourteen mailmen are dead. Six wounded."

"Jesus!"

"Fourteen dead!" I nodded gravely. "No one's ever come close to that."

"What happened to ol' Pat?"

"He shot himself in the head. A lot of them do."

"D'yer old man ever go off?"

"Huh?"

"Your old man ever go off?"

"Nah . . . but he should have."

"Is that right?"

"You better believe it."

"And why is that?"

" 'Cause he's such a psycho dick."

"Hmmph." Brady considered this for a moment. "So's my dad."

"I guess they all are," I said.

"Probably."

Career
Opportunities

The ones that never knock? Every job they offer? Like what? Mail clerk? Lawyer's assistant? Nonprofit organization paper filer? Turnip twaddler? Dishwasher? Telemarketing money beggar? Bike messenger? Retail clothes sales (I was certainly underpierced for record store employee)?

It seems once you've passed the age of twenty-five, Mrs. Field's cookie pusher is no longer an option. If I was buffed out a bit more, perhaps I might have scored a position at one of The City's many gay clubs as a stripper, but such was not my lot.

I worked in a restaurant that one winter with Callahan. The best thing was all the free gourmet food and it was always nice and warm in the kitchen after stepping in from the cold, wet, gray of outside. But the work was hellish. It was always so frantic, everyone racing around as though a jumbo jet had just crash landed and we were the rescue crew. It was why I jumped ship to work at the BagelWorks.

I could always work for BagelWorks's arch rivals in the Berkeley Bagel Wars of the Dawn of the Third Millennium, Bubi's Bagels. I'm sure they'd be very interested in some of the insider information I possess. You wanna know about the smoked salmon schmear? Let's talk.

My college degree? Apparently useless. It's not even absorbent enough for use as a place mat. I've looked in the paper. There's *never* any jobs listed under historian. I don't know what I was thinking when I chose my major.

Actually, I don't even want a job just yet (let alone a *career*), but unfortunately, the state requires I at least make a feeble attempt at finding work. My main plan is to apply for positions that I haven't the slightest chance of getting: Musical archivist for Geffen Records, taste tester at Anchor Brewery, booty tilter and tit tucker for *Sports Illustrated* swimsuit photo shoots, paid subject for an extensive study on napping, spokesperson for the cheese industry. Things like that.

Besides, I have other plans, bigger dreams. I possess a destiny of riches and fame, you know. It was revealed to me on the Ouija board up in Ole Sis's room back when I was ten. How I came by the riches and fame (obviously my college education is not involved) didn't concern me at the time. As the Ouija ruled in my favor, I merely shot Ole Sis the cocksure and cool look that only a prepubescent boy can master.

But now, well, I'm becoming a bit impatient. In an attempt to speed the process along, I have at least tried to imagine how I might achieve my great wealth and celebrity.

There was, of course, rock star. I *had* the records. The eclectic, well-informed, rageful tastes. I even had an acoustic guitar that sat in the corner gathering dust awaiting the next time I would pick it up for a frantic week of noodling (Dear Old Dad refused me an electric until I mastered the acoustic, which I never did, and, to this day, I blame *him* for my thwarted Rock God fantasies).

Movie star crossed my mind for a moment. I'm nearly short enough. Unfortunately, I'm far too withdrawn around strangers, and acting makes me feel uncomfortable.

Porno star. Admittedly, the level of fame and richness would be somewhat compromised, but I'd be getting thousands of times the sex while avoiding *all* of the dating.

Then there was my favorite. The purest and most direct deliverance of them all: Super Lotto Millionaire. Meet Steve Reeves, the latest Super Lotto Millionaire. I receive checks of $345,000 after taxes each and every year for a long time. They arrive in the day's mail sometime around spring, as the rosebuds swell with the coming summer. That would be the sweetest of all. Fuck all the struggling and work.

But, so far, all of the above has eluded me. The record contracts, the book deals, the Nobel Peace Prizes, the copious amounts of we-deliver sex from hot and nasty girls? Brick.

So let's move on to the other trouble spot in my life right now: women. My problems are twofold. First, I don't have a woman. Second, I don't know any. But once I removed my hands from my privates and ceased with the utterly impossible fantasy of many beautiful women living only to please me in an endless array of permutations and combinations, I decided to get down to business. I pulled out my old black book.

Rachel (the bitch!) and I had been going out for some eight months and seventeen days, so while the trail was, admittedly, cold, calling my bevy of old flames would at least not seem totally obvious. You know, just checking in on an old and dear friend. Keeping the friendship alive and vital. (In reality, as soon as I break up with a woman I do two things. Well, after the weeping and being bedridden, I do two things: First, I pretend that we're still friends, no hard feelings, the it's all good bit. Secondly, I make it a point to not only never speak to them ever again, but also quietly hope their lives are forever ruined.)

Until, of course, a day like today rolls along. The kind of day where an ex-girlfriend is a good thing.

I rang up the first candidate.

"Is Paula there?"

"Who?" It was a man's voice. A man whom I imagined had a gigantic beer belly and an overly tight, sweaty tank top.

"Uh . . . Paula?"

"There's no Paula here, pal."

OK, no problemo. I saw Sianna's name, but decided to save her for a later date. Not only did she live in San Diego, but the leather masks and bondage bit of hers was not quite my cup of tea. And then I saw Mimi's name. How about old Mimi?

It took me a couple of referrals, but I finally got her latest phone number.

"Could I speak with Mimi?"

"One sec, I'll get her. Hey! Mimi. Phone."

"Hello?"

"Mimi, how's it going? It's Steve."

A quickly excruciating silence followed, so I said, "Remember me? Steve . . . Reeves?"

"Steve? How did you get this number?"

"Well, your last roommate . . ."

"I've got a boyfriend, you know." CLICK.

Well, alrighty then. I moved down the list. How about Barb? Of course! Barbara and I had a pretty good thing going once. She was a smart, funny, multiorgasmic sword swallower. If it hadn't been for her rather heavy moustache and the fact that she already had a boyfriend, we might have had something longer lasting and more meaningful, but I kinda liked being a back door man. It was a role I turned out to be quite well suited for. The afternoon trysts up in her apartment, her boyfriend coming home from work in a couple of hours, almost getting caught a couple of times. I loved it. It was like James Bond without the weapons and gadgets, but then guilt set in. Barb couldn't handle the truth and it was quits. What has time wrought?

"Barbara?"

"Yes. Who is this?"

"It's Steve . . . Reeves."

"Oh, Steve, I don't believe it." She followed these words with that grunting scoff of hers, that full-body exhalation filled with desire and derision.

"Yeah, how you been?" I asked.

"Hmmm," I heard over the line and I remembered that hot lanky body of hers. "I been good. How you been?"

The way she said, "How you been?"—it was more of a "How *you* been?"—I immediately knew what she was talking about. She was asking about my package. The boys. My red-helmeted love gladiator. She wanted it. Barb was good to go.

"Good," I said. "Oh, it's been good."

"Listen, I can't talk right now, ya know . . . ?"

"Right," I said. I gotcha. The boyfriend. Barb was good to go! Right on! Life was again wonderful.

"Why don't you give me your number, and I'll call sometime," she offered. I did.

Okay. It was a fine day of unemployment. The wheels were now in motion.

Unemployment Days

I sat with my coffee and notebook at the café like any good unemployed artist. It was a caffe latte dopio alto skim milk jobber with chocolate powder on top and seemed to be hitting the spot. The open-air café made me feel like I was in Paris maybe except for that one street person who kept parading by every eleven minutes. The one that looks like Rasputin: long, disheveled gray hair; the thick Russian-winter beard; the ratty smocklike coat. He always walks about with his arms spread and his eyes skyward in what I take to be a highly religious pose. In fact, I don't see how he's avoided being hit by a Volvo station wagon by now. He never seems to watch where he's going. Perhaps, like the real Rasputin, he is somewhat indestructible.

I drank my coffee and the morning dose of caffeine filled me with a confidence, a joy, an optimism that I perhaps would not see again until the perfect beer moment passed over me sometime later that night at The Pub or The Yukon. That's when I noticed this girl.

She took a seat a couple of tables from mine. I happened to look up from my paper right as she sat down, and she smiled at me and I fumbled back *something* in return (*I'm* convinced it came off clumsy and stupid, that a lip-licking leer would have been an improvement) and then quickly looked back down at my paper. I don't know why I looked away so quickly, because that's what I do? That's what I've always done? I mean you can't keep staring, right?

I pretended to scribble a rough sketch of the Great American Novel in the notebook, but really was only thinking about this girl. I snuck occasional peeks her way. She was cute as hell and I was totally lost in Love and still had half a coffee as well as most of the newspaper so I was in for the ride.

She looked good in her shades, toying with her pen and notebooks. Her hair was long, a real light brunette or a dark blonde. She had a couple of long, tight braids, which I always fall for, and, along with the sunglasses, they really set off her small, round face. She had one of those little button noses that I'm no longer partial to, having been destroyed by sufficient Waspy women with upturned noses, but on this girl, on that morning, it looked good.

She had an especially dreamy mouth. The lips were thin, but they curved up at either end, and while I read about the A's and their crappy pitching, I was really just imagining what exactly that mouth might be capable of and how such a mouth might be just what my world needed right then.

She was probably a coed at Cal and now that I was long graduated, just the word "coed" carried with it an erotic charge that really didn't seem fair.

She looked up again and caught me. I was staring at her like I was a sculptor fashioning her likeness. The sort of stare that had an air of permanence to it. I reactively offered up a weak smile in my red-handedness. She smiled back and held my eyes in her own for an instant. Then we both looked down, and I was both embarrassed and aroused. Nothing came of it.

The Guns of Cedar Manor

The crusty old codger at Mission Control of the Lake Chabot Shooting Range sized us up and seemed none too pleased with what he saw. There was Brady, tattooed, pierced, chain-smoking, and angrily gulping bitter coffee out of a Styrofoam cup. Billy (who I don't think had been outside since Travolta was a sweathog) was decked out in full Hell's Angel regalia, his thin arms impossibly white, his entire body seeming to crumple under the weight of sunlight it hadn't seen in years. Myself? I was dressed in my latest Salvation Army outfit: a freshly pressed official Postal Worker short-sleeved shirt complete with Eagle shoulder emblem, circa mid-eighties. The Patrick Sherrill days.

"You boys got any ear protection?" the old guy asked.

"Huh?" I asked.

"Ear plugs, you boys got ear plugs?"

Billy reached into his pocket and pulled out a Plen-T-Pak of Juicy Fruit gum.

"Guess that'll do." The guy looked us over some more. "How 'bout eye wear? You boys got yourself eye protection?"

Billy pointed a thumbs-up at his headgear and attempted to smile. There was no questioning Billy's eye protection; he was wearing a pair of wraparound Blu-Blockers *underneath* a clear, shatter-proof, protective welder's hood–type face shield apparatus. I pointed at my glasses, and Brady reached into his pocket and pulled out a pair of those tiny colored swimming goggles and looked at us defensively.

"What? What, dude? It was all I had!"

"Hmmm . . ." The old guy was just not liking the idea of us on his shooting range with loaded weapons, so we quickly laid down our money, stepped back a couple of docile feet, and tried to look as angelic as possible.

"Well, all right. Here's your targets. Now, be careful." He pointed at each one of us individually. "No funny business out there. Guns are serious."

"That's what I was telling these boys." Billy made a lame attempt at passing himself off as the responsible one.

"Go on!" the codger ordered.

We were set up on table seventeen, and while Brady and Billy shot, I regaled the boys with one of my favorite tales of Postal Revenge Killings. The Joseph Harris Story.

> Reeves: So, Harris is getting pretty pissed off by now. Things aren't going well at the PO, his woman, this supervisor, has dumped his ass and taken up with another man. . . .

Billy: That's a fuckin' bitch for you, man.

Reeves: Billy, Harris is the maniacal killer in the story.

Billy: Yeah, right. Watch me cap old Tricky Dick.

Billy had smuggled in a vintage poster of Richard Nixon. An official one by CREEP, the Campaign to Re-elect the President. He had it rolled up in one of his rifle cases. The thing looked brand-new. Like it had just come off the press.

That day, I realized that Billy was possibly suffering from Korsakoff's syndrome. Time had simply stopped in Billy's mind. Reagan was still only governor, Hendrix and Zeppelin were the latest form of music, and he kept referring to the president as "that asshole Nixon." He absolutely refused to eat any of the donuts I'd brought that morning after he found out they were made by Asians.

"Get that raised glazed fuckin' away from me!" he yelled. "I ain't eatin' no fuckin' donuts made by Charlie."

Brady: Where'd ya get that poster, anyway?

Billy: That's just not any of your fuckin' business, Andy Boy.

Reeves: Anyway, Harris, the thing I love about this guy, he didn't kill that many coworkers, but . . .

Brady: How many?

Reeves: Four. Three postal workers and the supe's boyfriend.

Billy: Cool.

Brady: We cain't smoke here?

Billy: What?! DAMN! Motherfuckin' FOOL! What are you, shit for brains?

Brady looked at me and shrugged. Billy got up from the bench.

Billy: Your turn, Reeves.

Reeves (*taking a seat*): No, Brady. No smoking. Anyway! As I was saying, Harris is no Patrick Sherrill, but then, who is? But the great thing about Harris is, first off, he had a booby-trapped apartment. Homemade bombs . . .

Billy: The Shop's booby-trapped, you know.

Reeves: And his choice of weaponry might have been the most original of all Postal Revenge Killers.

Billy: I got stuff hidden in The Shop you don't ever want to come fucking face-to-face with.

Reeves: Can I tell this story?

Billy (*staring down Brady*): Oh, yeah. Better fucking believe it. Don't be tryin' nothin'.

Brady: What am I gonna be tryin'?

Billy: I ain't worried about *what* . . . just don't.

Reeves: LISTEN! Harris marched into his ex-girlfriend's apartment and, get this, he's wearin' a gas mask and a bulletproof vest and he's armed with a .22 machine pistol, a fucking Uzi, *grenades,* and a samurai sword. Can you believe that shit?!

I looked at them excitedly, expectantly. Dead silence.

Billy: You gonna fuckin' shoot that damn mother-fuckin' gun or not, Reeves?

Brady: Yeah, you're always talkin' about what a crack shot you are. Hittin' orange trees or some such shit.

Reeves: All right, motherfuckers.

I nestled the weapon against my shoulder. It was an old Ruger Mini-14, one of the first commonly available assault-type weapons, a more powerful version of the weapon Thomas McIlvane had found so useful at the Royal Oak PO. Billy had it specially rigged to handle this gigantic banana clip packed with infinite rounds of rapid-fire .223 ammo for those special firefights that he was sure might occur at any given moment. I centered the sights on the middle of Nixon's forehead, imagining that technically I was probably committing some federal offense against the presidency. I squeezed off a round.

Billy: You just nicked Dick's ear.

Brady: Big fuckin' deal. That ain't no shootin'.

The gun was shooting a couple of inches right, so I adjusted.

Reeves: I'm nailin' Nixon in the mouth 'cause he was a liar.

B & B: Yeah!

I squeezed off a round and the Mini-14 made a tiny pop compared to the loud explosions coming from the guys sighting in their deer rifles. Billy was spying through his spotting scope.

Billy: Damn, Reeves. Right in the mouth. You're the fuckin' outlaw spawn of maniacal mailmen, man.

Reeves: I told you, don't fuck with me.

Brady: Lemme see that gun!

Reeves: You wanna see shootin'? Wait till the pistols come out.

Billy: Yeah. Fuckin' YEAH!

Over at the pistol range, Billy pulled out of a Pony Express/Harley-Davidson leather satchel a pistol that looked like it might have once belonged to Billy the Kid. It was an ancient revolver with a barrel about two feet long. Nickel plate, checkered wood grips, iron bead at the end of the barrel as a sight.

Reeves: Damn, that's a nice gun, Billy.

Billy: Fuckin' A.

I pulled my shit out of its small leather case. The Colt's MK IV/Series '70 Gold Cup National Match .45 Auto. Gun black, checkered wooden grips, a bar and a notch fore and aft for sights. Grave and heavy. Perfectly balanced.

Billy: Lemme see that. That's fuckin' nice. Your old man gave you that?

Reeves *(nodding)*: Mailman gun.

Billy *(examining the pistol)*: Yeah.

Brady: Gimme that thing.

Billy: Wait a goddamned minute, Tex.

Brady: Now, why do ya gotta keep on callin' me Tex when I asked ya so many times not to?

Billy: Don't be gettin' ornery with me . . . Andy Boy, or I just might have to clip your wings.

Brady: Clip my wings?

Billy: Yeah, you know what that is?

Brady shrugged.

Billy: You know, College Boy?

Reeves: No idea, Billy.

Billy *(looking about suspiciously)*: It's a thing they used to do in the Angels. Sonny was what you might call a big fan of clippings.

Reeves: What is it?

Billy: It's when somebody gets outta line and you don't wanna kill the bastard, ya just wanna send a message to the fucker.

Brady: What's the dang message?

Billy: Fuckin' cool your jets is the message and I'll fuckin' tell you. Shit! What you do is you take the guy and you cap him three times with a small-caliber weapon, like a .22. Once in each shoulder and once *(laughing)* in the family jewel vault.

Reeves: The groin? Oh man, that's gotta hurt.

Brady: That's harsh, dude.

Billy *(nodding his head)*: Oh, yeah. Yeah it is.

The pistol range was great fun, and we quickly blasted our way through a few boxes of ammo. Brady was a pretty good shot, and Billy might have been all right if he could've held his hands still, but all the crystal kinda kept him a little too jittery for that. None of them, however, was a match for Son of a Mailman.

Dad's pistol felt very familiar in my hand, and by the second clip I was blasting the ten-ring with impunity. The gun also seemed to go well with my Postal shirt and all of it reminded me of when Dear Old Dad used to take the family shooting every now and then as a form of recreation. We'd all hop into the car and head east, over the Laguna Summit, past Buckman Springs, and then down, down into the Anza-Borrego desert.

I loved the desert. The jumbled rock landscape. The alien ocotillo waving strangely in the hot blasts of desert wind. I loved the heat. The intense dryness. The blazing sun. Cans of ice-cold Coke in the cooler.

Mom would always pack a picnic with sandies and cookies she'd just baked and the twelve-pack of Coors for Dad and the famous coleslaw, which Auntie taught all the family's womenfolk.

I liked to take off my T-shirt and put the neck over the crown of my head and loosen up the plastic tab on my baseball cap and put that on top to make a Lawrence of Arabia with bill action headgear. Then I'd walk into the desert.

"You be careful," Mom would say, sitting in the shade of the car, sipping her margaritas that she'd bring in a big thermos. Mom was only ready for the desert if she had her big thermos full of margaritas all mixed up perfect. In fact, the few times I ever saw Mom drunk was in the desert, sitting in the shade of the family car, in the blazing heat.

Off I'd walk into this blazing heat, in my Arab headgear, to just around that first jumble of rocks, with Mom's warning to be careful and maybe Ole Sis alongside. We couldn't wait to get past that first hill, out of sight of Dear Old Dad, who at some point on every family outing would go Postal. Actually, it was through Dad's screaming fits and the constant firing of rounds at last week's beer can collection that I became such a crack shot.

The Water
Conspiracy

In the days since I last enjoyed a gainful employment (a good six weeks have now passed), I've learned
three things.

First, Erica on *All My Children* is just *not* gonna
win an Emmy. So, give it up already, everybody.

Second, none of the women I have *ever* known are
ever going to call me back, so now I actually have to
go to the trouble of meeting someone brand-new (and
because Barb obviously lied about calling me back, she
has inadvertantly become an occasional subject of some
fantasies of a rather violent nature involving, of course,
the gun). That's the problem with getting dumped.
There's no backup system.

I dumped a girl once. Come on, it wasn't just *me*
getting trashed all the time. I'm just better trained for
it. Betrayal, rejection, anger, spite. It is these emotions
I have experience with. The tact, tenderness, and un-
derstanding required for a good dumping I just don't
have.

The one time I did it was at the Burger Depot. It was the closest I could come to something out of the movies like Bogart canning Bergman in *Casablanca*. Instead of a foggy airport, I was at the Burger Depot. Instead of arrivals and departures and the imminent appearance by the Nazis, there were mediocre shakes, greasy burgers, and the impending arrival of a stomachache.

The third conclusion I've come to, given all my leisure time, is that Mrs. Park is beginning to lose her mind. All she ever wants to talk about is the Water Conspiracy.

Mrs. Park is convinced that water is being diverted. That the precious liquid is being tampered with. That things that should be moist are suspiciously dry and things that should be dry are alarmingly damp.

Mrs. Park will materialize out of nowhere without a sound at any time of the day or night when you least expect it. "Oh, there you are," is always her greeting when it's *she* who miraculously appears out of thin air. You never hear a sound until her voice. Until she says, "Oh, there you are" and then launches into a discussion about the Water Conspiracy.

The strangest part is the hushed tone she uses whenever she describes to me in confusing detail the latest evidence she's uncovered regarding the evil rerouting of ancient and natural drainage patterns perpetrated, she's convinced, by the landlord Carp and his construction of the diabolical hot tub. I wish a cone of silence might be lowered down upon us as she looks about nervously before whispering the latest. I can barely hear her go on and on.

Before complete obsession set in, Mrs. Park ran a veritable dim sum factory out of her cottage that kept me well fed. She was always dropping off little plates of food: noodles with bits of five-spice chicken, a bowl of rice with bok choy and broccoli, crunchy little spring rolls, and the famous plums she gathered from around the neighborhood.

At first I always dutifully washed the plates and bowls after eating the incredible food. I'd carry them back to her cottage and knock on the door to thank her. She let me in twice, but always seemed ill at ease inside her own home, somehow at a disadvantage.

Her place was dark, the drapes always drawn. A museum clutter filled the entire living room: ancient books, antique furniture, small appliances in various states of repair, twigs and branches she gathered from around the neighborhood, which she fashioned into wreaths she sold at flea markets and yard sales. On an old end table there was a black-and-white photo of her standing before a stream in hip waders with a man I imagined to be her father. She was holding a very large king salmon. She was young and beautiful. Oval face, smooth porcelain skin, a lovely smile, and sweet almond eyes. She still had the same wonderful eyes and smile.

It was after one of these visits, after I'd knocked on the door and Mrs. Park answered, opening the door slowly, just a crack, to the limit of the chain. She'd look at me in an odd way, as though she'd just woken or didn't recognize me or needed glasses. Then she'd quickly shut the door and I'd hear the sliding of the chain. The door would reopen, and Mrs. Park would smile nervously.

Soon after, she told me to just leave the plates on my stoop. That she'd pick them up on one of her many walks. That I shouldn't trouble myself.

But now the food supply was beginning to dry up. And at the worst possible time, with me out of work and my bagels and smoked salmon long gone. All she cares about is the Water Conspiracy. Yesterday she even had a tool for her investigation. I was walking up the steps to the Manor, wondering how life might have turned out if, while I was still a toddler, Dear Old Dad had been kidnapped by aliens, anally probed, and whisked off to their faraway galaxy, when I heard a voice in my right ear.

"Oh, there you are." It was Mrs. Park. She was dressed in her usual uniform: baggy khaki pants, a long-billed Cal baseball cap on her head, and a pair of pruning shears in her hand, a pair of gum-soled gardening boots on her feet, and, if it was cool in the morning summer's fog or at dusk, her dark blue sweater, the one a couple of sizes too big (I think it might have belonged to her father) that she wrapped around herself and which, over the years, had taken on the appearance of a kimono.

Mrs. Park looked about her as though she was being followed and then lowered her voice and asked in an ominous tone, "Have you seen the backyard?"

"Umm, well no. Not exactly," I said. I had long since decided there was no water diversion conspiracy but didn't dare say as much since she held the idea so dear.

"It's quite wet," she said in a satisfied manner, as though DNA evidence had just arrived in the day's mail. "I think his hot tub, he doesn't have all the permits, you know."

"Yeah, what's with that hot tub, anyway? Are we gonna get to use it?" I asked.

Mrs. Park rolled her eyes and made a face. "Do you mind if I check behind your cottage?" She held up some sort of metal device which I'm fairly certain was a straightened clothes hanger mounted on a wooden handle, but which she wielded as a special wetness and water diversion measuring device.

"Why, no," I said. "Go right ahead."

"Okay, I'll let you know what I find."

Job Referral #1

My evil seed I was telling you about before, if you were fucking listening, was on my mind this morning. I have become convinced that this evil seed was planted deep within my being at a very early age by Dear Old Dad. I have no concrete evidence, of course, but *I'm* convinced, and that's all that matters. Don't question my authority! Question, instead, why? Why did Daddy plant this evil family seed in his one and only boy? Was it the result of the blame he placed on everyone for his thoroughly unsatisfying life? Was it the bitterness he held so dear? Was it the disappointment that tainted all he came into contact with? Was it simply something to do with the United States Post Office? I don't know, but I sincerely believe that I was hatefully prepared. My father's seed, the single sperm that found its mark, was a malcontent. Disgruntled. Possibly Evil.

Perhaps this evil runs far deeper than simply Dear Old Dad. Perhaps we possess a family curse of historical proportions. Perhaps Dad is merely the personification of *his* father's Karma: Old Grampa smuggled into the country in a banana boat from Ecuador (the family name actually being Rivas). Maybe Grampa was infected with an evil seed from up in the fucking Andes, stretching back to the days of Pizarro! What if that were the case? Can there be any escape for me, or is Fate an iron-fisted, unforgiving mistress?

I had no chance to answer these and many other important questions because my bus had reached its stop, and it was time to go to a job interview the Employment Development Department had helpfully provided to set me on the path of economic recovery. The truth is, I don't *want* my employment developed. Developed employment is the *last* thing I want, but go I must or the state cuts me off. The state *is* an iron-fisted and unforgiving mistress. And at $104 a week, a cheap one, too.

It seems my one gig as a prep cook and my bagel boiling experience has convinced The State that I possess culinary aptitude; they've given me a list of restaurant jobs. I've yet to be sent out on the much-hoped-for swordfishing expedition.

I sat at a table in the dining room of a restaurant filling out an application with a felt-tipped pen. I possessed neither résumé nor ballpoint. I began the process greatly disadvantaged.

Just the thought of filling out the application gave me a sick, hollow feeling in the pit of my stomach. The hairs on the back of my neck stood at attention, and I felt a brief wave of nausea. I began to get writer's block as I tried to remember what subjects I studied in elementary school. Why don't they ever ask about my wonderful *college* education?

The only other people in the dining room were the

chef, who angrily threw me this application when he found out I didn't *have* a résumé, and a cook, whom the chef was in the process of reaming a new asshole. There seems to have been a problem with the day's corn pudding.

"I'm not saying you're stupid." The chef began to raise his voice. "I just said you have to get your shit together."

"Well, I understand," the cook dared to speak, "I just . . ."

"No! I don't think you *do* understand. If you understood, the corn pudding wouldn't have been burnt."

It was obvious from the screaming going on between the cook and chef that this was the HMS *Bounty* of restaurants. I felt embarrassed for us all, yet continued with the application. The elementary school section was a hopeless mess (the clumsy felt-tipped pen unable to squeeze all the subjects into the tiny line provided), so I skipped to the job experience section.

"Look, you were better on your first night here," the chef continued. "It's like you're getting worse."

"It's only been a week. In a year I'll have it down."

"A year?! I don't have that long. Don't you see? It's the snowball effect."

Why do they always ask about hobbies and activities on these applications? I'm not joining their glee club. I'll put down: stalking supermodels. See if anyone notices.

"The snowball effect?" the cook asked.

"Yeah, you put the custards in too late and then turned up the oven to speed things up. What happens? The corn pudding's burnt. See what I mean?"

"The snowball effect?"

"Yes! And it's my job to see where the snowball starts. Understand?"

"Uh . . . yeah, or it just keeps getting bigger?"

"Exactly! Now get back in that damn kitchen. There's a lot of work to do. You better be ready when the shit hits the fan."

I came to the question on the application I hated most: Why did you leave your last job?

After learning about the snowball effect, I decided, for once, to be honest and wrote down: I left because the boss was almost as big an asshole as *you* appear to be.

Cows upon the Chaparral

The phone rang suddenly as it will after sitting there dead silent for nine days. After I got over the shock, I sprang toward it, eager and hopeful, with visions of a pleading, weeping Rachel dancing through my head. It was Ole Sis.

OS: Steve?

S: Sis?

OS *(laughing)*: Yeah?

S: Oh, what's up?

OS: Oh, nothing. Just thought I'd give you a call. See how things were.

S: Fine. What's new with you?

OS: Oh, nothing. Doug's just getting the nursery ready.

S: That's cool. Uh, when's the due date?

OS: Ten more weeks.

Her voice climbed the scale as she said it. I could hear the distinct pleasure in it, and I began, again, to feel that free-falling anxiety.

OS: Doug's been building a crib, you know.

S: Mmmm.

OS: So, what's new with you?

Funny she should ask. That very morning I had decided to become more productive. No more simply sucking up a huge coffee and a sugar- and fat-laden pastry. (Oh, sure, a fucking couple of slugs of Peet's coffee and a power scarf of a chocolate croissant and I'm fucking Superman, but it's all rather short lived. Fifteen minutes later, I'm walking my cottage in the dazed state of a plane crash survivor suffering from a mild head injury, or I'm overcome with the gnawing anxiety of someone marooned on a desert island with limited prospects for rescue.) No, this morning I actually had a glass of orange juice and some toast and then jotted down a small list of things I wanted to accomplish today. Nothing too long. I'm so easily discouraged these days. Today's list:

1. Superglue the locks to the BagelWorks.
2. Make constant phone calls to Shorter (I have his home phone number) and then hang up.
3. Make constant phone calls to Rachel and then hang up.
4. Drop by the back door of the Chicken Shack and see if Brady can't slip me some day-old O. G.
5. Start my new Beef up for Babes exercise program.

S: Oh, been doing a little working out.

OS: Yeah? Running?

S: A little. Mostly working with free weights.

Actually, the extent of my four-hour-old exercise program was nine push-ups. I looked at myself in the mirror to check the rippled form of my bulging biceps. They seemed about the same, but I can't expect to pump myself up to the size of the Original Recipe Steve Reeves overnight. Either way, I promised myself not to invest too much into this project. My new motto is: I wasn't really trying. This, I figure, will save me from the embarrassment of nearly any failure.

OS: That's good.

S: I've also been working on a new campaign for the Pear Council.

OS: The Pear Council?

S: Yeah, you know, like the Egg Brigade or those almond guys with their "Just one can is all we ask?" How 'bout this: Pears, fruit's answer to the potato?

OS: Huh?

S: Okay, wait, how 'bout: Pears, the potato of the fruit world?

OS: I don't get it.

S: Never mind.

OS: Oh, Doug wants to talk to you.

S: Huh?

D: Steve, how's it goin' up in Frisco?

S: Well, actually, I live in Berkeley.

D: Yeah, listen, I talked to my friend, Dwight. He can maybe hook you up.

S: Hook me up?

D: Yeah, at the wedding you were saying how you'd like to get a PO job.

S: Huh?

D: So, I gave him your number. He might be giving you a call.

S: You gave him my number?

D: No problem. That's what family's about.

S: But . . . thanks.

D: Here's Kim.

OS: Wasn't that nice of Doug? I think he really likes you.

S: Great. Any other surprises down there?

OS: Well . . . we're thinking of getting a cow.

S: What?!

OS: We might get a cow.

S: A cow? Isn't it kinda hot out there for a cow?

OS: No.

S: What the hell are you going to do with a cow?

OS: So the baby can learn about animals and stuff.

S: I don't get it. How'd you come up with a cow?

OS: There's nothing wrong with cows.

S: Why not a nice cat?

OS: I don't like cats and we *had* dogs.

S: Don't remind me.

OS: It wasn't our fault. Jeez!

S: Awright, awright.

OS: Oh, before I forget. Mom and Dad are thinking of coming up to visit.

S: What?!

OS: Didn't Mom call you?

S: No . . . No!

OS: I think the weekend after next. You better call her.

A cow? Random calls from some mailman I don't even know? Mom and Dad coming up to visit? What the fuck's going on down there? The cow thing, I later realized, was probably some warped vestige of Ole Sis's Heidi fantasies. It'd be one thing if she lived in Wisconsin or something, like Mom's family, but she lived about thirty-five miles east of San Diego. Jackrabbits and coyotes are challenged to eke out a living out there. Illegal immigrants die trying to traverse the harsh, dry landscape. How can a cow possibly survive? It's gonna be like the dogs all over again.

Right after she moved in with Doug, Ole Sis had planned a move up to rural Oregon and a real farm where she could have goats and sheep and cows. Unfortunately, Doug was unable to get a transfer (this, I imagine, immediately marked his supervisor for later annihilation). So Ole Sis settled on a dog. Well, not *a* dog, five of them at once. All shapes and sizes. Doug constructed a row of kennels in which to incarcerate the animals because Ole Sis had decided it was bad for dogs to interact or roam free.

The dogs were locked in their pens where they remained 23.5 hours each and every day. A bowl of water and a plate of food was slid under the door every evening at five o'clock. Two of them would growl when approached, while the other three wagged their tails—their entire bodies—in anticipation and jumped against the chain-link door of the kennel, hoping for much more than anyone could offer.

Finally, after a few months of lockdown, the Siberian husky, unable to withstand the one hundred-degree summer weather in his thick coat, developed some sort of virulent Ebola-mange that soon swept through the kennels. By September, the entire lot of them had to be put down.

So what does Doug think about The Bovine Thing? Well, despite being the walking time bomb that *is* a United States Postal Worker, at home Doug is like Burundi in the United Nations. His vote doesn't count for very much. Only Ole Sis has veto power.

If Doug and I were on more intimate terms, I might be able to take him aside one fine afternoon, perhaps after a couple of beers and a good game of NFL football. We could step outside to the dried-up chaparral backyard of their house, marvel at the big pink rocks everywhere, our Budweisers tucked into their foam cozies, and I could say, "G, whaz up with ya' ho?" But, alas, we are not so close.

Besides, the possibility of my parents visiting is a much more disturbing prospect and must be discouraged at all costs. I now realize that 600 miles is not distance enough to escape from them for say . . . five years? Perhaps a different time zone or entirely new continent is what's called for.

Where would they possibly stay? What could I possibly do to entertain them? How will I pretend to have a job? It's all so vexing and troublesome. I can't handle Dear Old Dad for an hour over dinner. What will an entire weekend be like? I'll tell you, it'll be like three days in a decompression chamber. Like a diver who's risen too fast from the depths, my life will flash before my eyes. I'll appear dazed and confused. My head will ache, and Mom will ask, "How is everything? Are you okay? Is everything all right?"

Rent

It was the fifth of July and there was no way around it. Rent was due. Unfortunately, that morning, I had been doing a bit of accounting, and things just weren't adding up. I had it all laid out on the table. The calculator was primed and ready, pencils sharpened to razor points, a stack of final notices on the left, my four-digit ATM bank balance cards (I'm counting the pennies as digits, by the way) at my right, and a big cup of steaming coffee. All to reach a conclusion that just can't exist: namely, that I'm pitifully broke.

Money was fucking me up. It was fucking me up good. I could hardly think of anything without money getting involved. There were times I'd catch myself seething and raging about the shit. It was beginning to get in the way of my fantasies of new love found (the tearful reunions with Rachel giving way to the fantasies involving Christy Turlington giving way to wondering about the satisfaction level of hiring a hooker: pleasure minus disease potential divided by cost).

See?! Back to money. I needed it! A good pile of it. Anything to avoid the situation that money condemns us all to: a full-time position. A crappy little jobby job.

Two facts summed up my cash flow problem. Number one was that unemployment checks came to $416 a month. Combined with number two, a monthly rent of $375, you can now appreciate my bind. We haven't even factored in beer and drugs, let alone food. And yet . . . an obvious solution sat right there before me: remove rent, and I could live like a king.

I considered the Colt nestled in its leather case, hidden deep within my closet under piles of ancient dirty underwear and cheesy socks. What if instead of walking over to Cottage C and paying Carp, I simply walked over there and capped his fat ass? That's an immediate savings of $375! The bonus being that he deserves to die anyway.

The catch? Without even getting into a moral debate, let's consider my near instantaneous arrest and subsequent incarceration at San Quentin where, on my first afternoon in Cell Block A, I become bitch to Bunny, a 6' 6" shaved-head motherfucker covered in tattoos. What then?

I immediately realized that I was far too frail to get my butt plowed on a daily basis and resentfully decided to pay Carp the rent.

I knocked rather sheepishly on Carp's door. Nothing. I knocked again. No answer. For a moment, I fantasized that this meant rent wasn't due until next month, but then I decided I better check out back.

As I suspected, Carp was out back overseeing the construction of his demonic hot tub. He was wearing a slightly yellowed tank top that he'd somehow stretched over his amazingly round torso along with a pair of ridiculous Hawaiian print shorts. His legs were impossibly pale and doughy and he was covered in his usual film of oily perspiration.

As I approached, I noticed he wasn't wearing any shoes. This has gone too far, I thought, as I surveyed the piss-colored calcified toenails that were disturbingly reminiscent of ten tiny Fritos.

It's so strange. He didn't seem half bad the first time I met him, back in the grand old days when he happily walked me through Cedar Manor. My life shined back then. It was always a sunny day, I liked to imagine. Rachel and I were still new and blossoming and the job at the 'Works remained only *poised* to ruin everything.

I remember Carp's smile and the rolling of his fingers. It seemed almost charming. He was like a bearded Tweedle-dee and the rent was cheap. A place all my own.

But first impressions, you know how they sometimes work out. Carp turned out to be a hippie gone sour. Someone left his cake out in the rain and I don't think that I can take it. He's one of those Volvo assholes I was telling you about (though in Carp's case, the Volvo was a disintegrating '75 station wagon hooptie). The kind of guy who has an "Arms Are for Hugging" bumper sticker and cuts you off in traffic.

"I got the rent," I said.

"Huh?!" Carp turned abruptly as though he'd been caught red-handed. "Oh, yes." An evil grin appeared on his round, bearded face, and his fingers began to roll in anticipation of the money they'd soon get to touch. "Do I need to check my calendar or could today be the fifth?"

"Mmmm." I smiled and began a slow confused

mime of looking about my person for the rent money. "Now where did I put that money? Hmm . . . uh-oh."

Carp, who had almost begun to drool, looked a bit crestfallen for a moment. I waited as he began to puff up and ready himself for a confused speech about rent and responsibility, when I magically produced the envelope.

"Oh! Here we go," I said.

He greedily took the envelope and tore it open. Then he licked the thumb of his right hand and began to count the money. I stood there filling with loathing and disgust.

My hate for Carp (well beyond the usual immediate crystalline heartfelt anger all rent collectors elicit in me) cannot be explained rationally, but there it was again: full-blown, fierce, and instinctual. An on-sight disgust that in all of my dealings with him, Mr. Carp had done nothing but reinforce.

His hypocritical smile. His conniving brain he thought to be so sly but that sat obvious beneath his bald and sweaty dome. The beady eyes and hawkish nose. The insatiable way in which he now counted my crumpled tens and twenties. It all contributed to an air of unctuousness that had me convinced he'd been concocted by Satan himself. That Carp had crawled out of a vat of Hell's own baby lotion.

"Looks like it's all here." Carp smiled like we were fucking buddies and dabbed his buttery forehead with a raggedy handkerchief as he sucked down the remainder of a Häagen-Dazs ice cream bar.

"Uh . . . so how's the hot tub coming?" I asked.

"Oh, just fine." Carp's face broke out in a smile far too large.

"That'll sure be nice this summer," I added hopefully.

Carp said nothing, a fat grin pasted on his face. This smile gave me the distinct feeling that a summer full of hot tub parties might not be taking place. Carp then let out The Wheeze and asked, "So how are things with you?"

"Far out," I said, in no mood for The Wheeze. "Gotta go. Later."

Carp had this wheeze. This tuberculoid sound I noticed my first week at the Manor. I had my bedroom window open and thought there was an asthmatic racoon choking on food in the backyard, but I soon found out that none of Nature's creations could produce such a sound. No, only the beast called Carp could emit such a troublesome emission.

The Wheeze was subliminal in the sense that if I had my window closed or the stereo on or the water running, the sound disappeared. It slipped your mind and then you might imagine that maybe, at long last, Thank Jesus! Thank the Lord! it had finally stopped. But this was never the case. As soon as quiet again settled over my cottage, there it was: Hurheeeh. Hurheeeh.

Compounding matters was an inexplicable ultra-sensitivity I somehow developed to the sound of Carp's rattling. Inexplicable because I don't have very good hearing. My left ear is particularly weak due to a cold I once had as a toddler that blew out the eardrum. In fact, I once impregnated a girl not because of my massive count of beefy and potent sperm, but rather, because I misheard "Don't come inside . . ." as an invitation, but I'd rather not discuss that here. Just know that I could hear Carp's cough like no one else. It became like Poe's "Tell-Tale Heart." I was acutely aware and being driven slowly mad.

But then, a miracle took place. As I got to know Carp, with each added repulsive detail (his rent greed, his reluctance to make any repairs, his constant noise complaints, all the usual things that make landlords so effortlessly repugnant), The Wheeze came to be my sole ally against him. It all happened in a flash. I simply decided The Wheeze was final proof that Carp was suffering a slow, painful, and lonely death.

Job Referral #2

It seems the State of California is even more desperate than I am. How else to explain the latest job development program flyer they've sent me? Nursing Home Floor Staff. What the fuck were they thinking? I can see it now, my brilliant career. One that will afford me a steady income at a relatively low wage for a minimum of effort.

The brochure screamed at me like one of those sorry ads they have on daytime TV for losers like me. The ones for bartending school or automotive mechanic.

Yes, that's right, a career in the nursing home industry. Today there are more old geezers than ever before, and the number will only increase over the next few decades. As a result, the demand for trained nursing home assistants has never been greater.

If you like old people, can master a mop, and don't mind changing the soiled bedsheets of a seventy-two-pound, eighty-four-year-old woman, then a career in the nursing home industry could be just what you've been looking for.

You'll meet and work with exciting professionals in the health care field. You'll cut a dashing figure as you wait for the bus in your rest home–issued leprechaun green hospital garb.

Impress your friends as you regale them with tales of midnight snafus, particularly messy bed soilings, the time you switched old man Thomas's pills and the codger actually tore off his cloth straitjacket and sprang over the bed railing, only to break his hip!

And the best part is, you're your own boss. You wield ultimate power in the quiet late-night corridors of Wing C. The Wrath of God awaits any Alzheimer's-addled oldster who doesn't understand the meaning of your command to "Shut up!"

You're probably thinking, sounds great, but how can a person like me, one bill away from the street and not quite in complete control of my emotions, get a job like that?

Easy. The Rechtlich School of Nursing Home Attendants. For a nominal fee, you can enroll and be trained by seasoned professionals who know the ins and outs of this exciting and expanding field of employment. Best of all, there are no requirements. No need for pesky diplomas, not even a high school one! All you need is $89.99 and a desire to become part of a caring and trained team of dedicated health care workers.

Get a job.

Help an old person.

Call Rechtlich.

I decided to go visit Billy instead.

Callahan

There'd been a time when summers were the sweetest days of all. When freedom was strong and the sun shone endlessly. When the water off La Jolla Shores warmed and the seaweed twisted about your ankles as the waves drew back into the sea, the water slurping and the little round rocks rolling in a clatter back into the break.

But this summer sputtered along with a tenuous shy sun never sure enough to beat back the fog. It sputtered along, as did my infinite unemployed days, until it finally settled, as all listless things finally will, in a tepid swirling slipstream spinning endlessly to nowhere, to a languid boredom puncuated by sharp stabbing moments of fear, loneliness, and Postal rage.

First off, my dating hadn't been going well at all. I did actually get this one chick's phone number. We talked a couple of times on the phone and then set up a date and I'm lovin' life imagining some fresh new shit is just what I need and then she doesn't show! She calls me up the next day and says she's so very sorry, some serious fucking shit came up in her life and so we set up another date and she says she can't wait and then? She doesn't show again! She calls me up and profusely apologizes and even has a bouquet of flowers delivered to Cottage A, front stoop (now Mrs. Park thinks I'm dating the sweetest girl the world has ever known and I haven't even gone fucking out yet!). She's triply sorry now, of course, but a complication of the original seriousness came up and she promises to make it up to me (this comes complete with undeniable sexual healing overtones in her voice) come Thursday. Of course she doesn't show again and I call her up to really let her have it (I even have a list made of the faults I think she might be most self-conscious about so as to get her real good), but she's not home. Her "sister" answers. A sister I've never heard mention of before and it sounds suspiciously like the chick, but now I figure if she's impersonating a make-believe sister, she's more fucked up than me, so I hang up the phone r-e-a-l slow and wonder, momentarily, if she might not now pull some sort of *Fatal Attraction* bullshit, but then relax in my chair, comforted by the fact of the Colt in my closet and what a good shot I am. I even work out a couple rough fantasies involving her coming over crazy as shit and me being forced to shoot her. It's ruled justifiable homicide. I end up fucking my lawyer, a Marcia Clark type, except blonde and even hotter.

So I was actually excited when I received a call from my long-lost buddy, Sherman Callahan, and accepted an invitation from my bisexual friend. *Secretly* bisexual, that is (possibly secretly homosexual). It was hard to tell, what with it being a secret and all.

Sherman Callahan was just back in town and invited me to this pub that calls itself The Pub because it worships all things English and Callahan, while being secretly bisexual (possibly secretly homosexual), was openly Anglophilic.

I first met Callahan at The Pub a couple of years earlier. The first sight I had of Sherman Callahan was of this strange young man walking down the avenue. He was quite a sight, it being a warm day in May and here was this guy walking down the street in a complete suit and tie affair. Maybe in San Francisco; not in Berkeley. Our eyes met, and he immediately and nervously diverted his to the sidewalk and brought his hand to his chin in what I then took to be a quite affected pose. Berkeley being full of poseurs, one had to be careful.

I returned to my paper and caffe latte. The mayhem was deliciously numbing that day. Ten-year-olds were dropping five-year-olds out of fourteenth-story windows for refusing to steal. Hundred Year Floods were occurring on a monthly basis. There was the tease of a possible unleashing of top secret biological warfare CIA experiments from some compound in the green valleys of Connecticut. The head researcher had gone to New York City for the weekend (possibly contaminated! my paper intrigued shamelessly) and now they're looking for him and he's probably in a shitload of trouble.

As I sipped my coffee and took in the day and felt that first drop of free-falling anxiety that is produced when you realize suddenly, helplessly, that the entire world is falling apart, I heard a voice.

"Scrabble?"

I looked up, startled, and there stood the figure from the street. The guy in the suit. He held a box of Scrabble under one arm.

"Uh, sure," I answered because, if nothing else, I

cannot fend off the unwanted attention of intruding strangers.

He sat down and set the board and his pint of ale upon the table. "I didn't get your name," he said as he began flipping the wooden Scrabble tiles.

"Uh, Steve. Steve Reeves. You can call me Reeves."

"Hunh. The Italian Hercules, right? My name's Sherman Callahan. Everyone calls me Cal." The hand he extended was long-fingered and somewhat bony, yet he grabbed mine firmly. He then looked down and stroked his chin and pursed his lips.

From that moment on, his gestures forever fascinated me. For a while I imagined that I could calculate his moods and thoughts from them, that I could gauge whether he was in one of his expansive jovial moods or one of his petty bitchy ones depending on how he held his chin and whether or not it came *after* an adjustment of his small, wire-rimmed glasses or *before* a smoothing back of his fine brown hair.

It was all you had to work with because Sherman Callahan (who could talk for hours, could pontificate onward, his father a lawyer you see) never told you *anything* about himself. All you had were those gestures and the fact that he had dropped out of Cal (hence his shame in being known as Cal) to become the first first-born male child in the long-lined Callahan clan from back near Boston way, the first since the Civil War or some such shit to not become a lawyer. That and the sneaking suspicion that he was secretly bisexual (possibly secretly homosexual) was all you had.

My laissez-faire schedule of unemployment allowed me to arrive at The Pub early and I had the Scrabble board ready and was into my first pint, waiting for Callahan with not a small amount of trepidation.

Callahan was one of those friends. A heroin among buddies. Fascinating on first impression, only to reveal a tar pit of human frailty, a black hole of neuroses.

And me! Why, I'm fucked up enough on my own. How can I bear the added weight of another's problems? Though, admittedly, sometimes it does take you away from your own tragedies for a bit. It's part of the reason I go and visit Billy. Just the sight of his wrecked existence—and him some twenty years older—often made me feel a little better about myself. Perhaps a visit from Cal was just the tonic I needed. Nothing like a spot of Schadenfreude on a fine July afternoon when you're feeling out of sorts.

"I see you've got the Scrabble ready," a voice said with some disdain. It was Callahan, fully materialized from memories near forgotten. A flesh-and-blood revelation fraught with strange anxiety.

"Cal." I got up, my arms spread in genuine joy of not having seen him in four, five months. I stood in heartfelt, open-armed, unreceived hug stance.

"No, no please." Callahan backed away jokingly. "I couldn't possibly relate to you the utterly inconsequential viability of these tiny bergs. Heartland?! By a thread!" And he held his thumb and forefinger close. "A thread!"

As usual, I didn't really know what the fuck he was talking about. I *knew* he'd just returned from some little town in the middle of nowhere. For reasons I had yet to fathom, Cal, in the dead of a tenuous Berkeley winter, would up and go.

The past January I had dropped him off at the downtown Oakland bus station. It was like some dangerous ghost town. Boarded-up shops and shabby buildings condemned from the earthquakes. Crack dealers and jacked prostitutes.

Callahan had his one saggy bag of luggage sitting at his feet. He was in his fancy fading clothes. Cal had all the finer things, but they were getting a little frayed at the edges: the Ferragamo shoes now scuffed, the stained French silk shirts, the old wool overcoat that probably fit him quite well in high school.

We were at that bus stop and Callahan was telling me how he just had to go. How he couldn't stand living up on the hill with Dad the Lawyer anymore. He'd blown himself out of his latest restaurant job and it was time to get out of town. His voice betrayed that h-hitch of his when he told me, "I g-gotta go."

And he'd go to the strangest places. Places like Laramie and Cody, Caspar and Ninilchik, winter in the U.P. He always promised a postcard, but it never came. It was as though he completely vanished off the face of the earth until one day a call came and Callahan was back in town.

Cal was well into his second pint and had beat me at the first game of Scrabble because he was some sort of idiot savant at the game. He'd constantly rearrange his tiles like some mad adding machine. Click clack clickity click clack, they'd go, his brow knitted, then he'd lay down a word like "zephyr."

As we set up the second game, I heard a "Shit, you faggots playin' some lil' bitch games or sumpin'?" and of course it was Brady and I cringed in the face of the sharply honed PCness of the crowd at The Pub as they shot us dirty looks and I felt worse still for my buddy Cal who, as I was saying, was secretly bisexual (possibly secretly homosexual).

"Who's the Marlboro Boy?" Cal asked and set down seven tiles. Presage. "Let's see, that's twenty-six points and fifty bonus points."

127

"Shit! That's Brady. He moved into that Pakistani freak's cottage last month," I said as I laid down some word like "cat" or "big." "He's from Texas."

"No shit," Cal said tartly.

" 'Sup, dude?" Brady smiled and pulled up a chair. I performed the introductions and Cal asked Brady if he wanted to play.

"No, dude. Board games give me the creeps. Makes me feel like I'm getting arthritis or sumpin'. Cain't get it up no more, ya know?"

"Not exactly," I said.

"Reeves says you're from Texas," Cal said.

"San Angelo. Know it?"

"I'm familiar with its facility. My father's lawyerly largess requisitioned summer visits to this place called Balmoria, I believe." Cal rubbed his chin carefully and then removed his glasses to clean them. "It had what was allusively the largest man-made pool in the world."

"Oh, dude! That big pool. I been there!" Brady exclaimed.

"Really?" Cal smiled and put his glasses back on.

"Yeah, middle of nowhere." Brady turned to me, "Rock sides, coupla diving boards. I think it even had fish in it, dude."

"Yeah, that's the place," Cal agreed.

"So what's your story?" Brady asked.

"I just got back from Hibbings. Hibbings, Minnesota. I was sequestered there for a remnant of the winter."

"That must have been cold as shit, dude," Brady said.

"Very." Cal nodded seriously and readjusted his glasses. He seemed pleased that survival of a Hibbings winter had elevated him in Brady's eyes. I wasn't sure if Brady had granted grudging approval or decided Callahan was simply a fool.

"B-but the spring," Callahan continued and I caught a fractional glimpse of the childhood stutter that Callahan kept buried, the corpse only emerging when he got emotional. "I th-think it was the most beautiful sight I've ever seen."

"Hmmph." Brady shoved his baseball cap back off his brow. "I'm gonna get me a beer. Anybody want one?"

"So what's with him?" Callahan asked as Brady went to fetch the beers.

"Uh, I don't know. He's pretty cool. Works at the Chicken Shack. I get all the free tainted chicken I can eat."

"He a big *ladies*' man?"

"Huh?"

"Chicks dig him?" Callahan spit the word "dig" out of his mouth like it was a bug in his food.

"I don't know, man," I said. "I only worry about whether chicks dig me."

"Mmmm." Callahan nodded conspiratorially.

After the games, Brady went on his way, and Cal and I jumped in The Car and labored our way up Marin Avenue to his dad's house up on Grizzly Peak. I liked to force The Car up the steepest street in the whole Bay Area as punishment for being so lame in the first place. At one point, as The Car rattled up toward the top, I was sure I detected the special odors and clacking sounds combination that signals expensive damage and imminent engine explosion, but we made it to the top, and Cal and I were glad and cheered The Car on as we pulled onto the street where Old Man Callahan lived. To the house where Cal grew up.

"I can't wait to see your dad," I said. Cal threw me a smirk followed by a slight lifting of the eyebrows with a minute curling of the lips on the left side. I took this to mean, "Gee, I'm so happy for you."

I was soon sitting in that sweet backyard of Old Man Callahan. The one that overlooked the whole bay. You could set your sights down to practically San Jose and north to the clear skies over the shadowed purple mountains that heralded Marin. The City. Both bridges. You could see it all from up there.

The fog hung behind the Golden Gate and the patio was still sunbaked and warm. Old Man Callahan had the barbecue going, and we were all sipping glasses of ten-year-old Napa Cabernet. The old man had popped it open special upon seeing me.

"No, no, I insist," he said as he handed me the ruby-filled glass. "Chateau Montelena. I think you'll like this."

And so I did. I always loved it up on the hill at Old Man Callahan's. Old Man Callahan, who wasn't really all that old, that's just what we all called him, was some mega-liberal lawyer. Went to Harvard, I think. Had the big bushy hair and the Boston accent. It was as though there was a brother younger than Teddy Kennedy. A secret younger Kennedy brother hidden all these years up on the hill in Berkeley. A small-framed, secret younger Kennedy brother with the same appetite for liquor and the good life.

If nothing else, I always looked forward to a visit simply for the food and drink. Smoked sturgeon with sourdough batards. Vintage ports. Little poussin we'd roast on the barbecue. He had old Pommards and lively young Beaujolais. One time Old MC even busted out lobsters and vintage Cliquot.

At Old Man Callahan's, for once the four-dollars-a-twelve-pack beer and bean burritos were put aside. The old man would pop the corks and fill the glasses and chat with us for a while (Callahan the Younger later telling me how a seemingly innocent statement by his dad was really some thinly disguised torture comment on him) and then he'd fill his glass and retire to his room with an "I'll leave you gentlemen to your conspiracies," a mischievous smile on his face, and the rest of the bottle on the table for us.

In the course of an evening, Callahan the Younger and Old Man Callahan *did* have their little endless jousting dramas over Cal's dropping out and forever shaming the family name, but it was just more of Gramma's anti-Semitism to me. It never really affected me directly, and Old Man Callahan was always quite gracious to me and held in high esteem the fact that I had a college degree. In fact, Old Man Callahan was really the *only* person who called me "College Boy" with any real affection.

I thought the guy was great, and whenever Cal got too hard ragging on his dad, I would always offer the fantasy trade of fathers like we were Big League owners and could trade them like second-string point guards.

That day, the bill of fare included lamb chops. Tiny, succulent lamb chops covered with fresh rosemary and olive oil and grilled rare on his barbecue and little new potatoes with parsley washed down with a Chateauneuf-de-Pape.

"I hope your lamb is cooked right," the old man politely asked.

"Mmmph, yash." I nodded while I scarfed away like someone just rescued after months in a Peruvian prison. Callahan the Younger picked at the food as though it were *just* passable, while I gnawed at that lamb chop, sucking away on the tiny bone as though I might never again see such a meal. My face glistened with juicy lamb fat and I delicately licked my fingers clean.

This is the life, I thought. I sipped my wine as the fog drifted in across the bay and the sun dipped into the Pacific. Tiny blasts of moist, sea-touched wind blew into the hill and across my face, while major chunks of my life seemed to resemble something out of a Dostoyevsky novel. In a way, I had almost all I needed, and in this comfortable poverty, the juicy little chops and aged wines were especially delectable.

Homo, P.I.

A few days later, Brady came over to my place with a couple of boxes of bacteria-laden, extra-crispy Chicken Shack legs and thighs.

I had been working on a list, listening to some particularly evil music. Black Sabbath or Ministry. I was going to call the list: Those Who Need to be Slaughtered, but thought better of it. I settled on: Enemies of the Realm. So far it had Shorter, Dad, Carp, Rachel/ Rich, Jay Leno, Barb (she *still* hasn't called back), the cast of *Friends*, Christian Slater (for daring to fuck Christy Turlington), every single band member of Oasis, Newt Gingrich, and that guy who killed Dahmer. What I'll ever do with this list I cannot say, but I'm keeping it around just in case.

"What you workin' on, dude?" Brady asked.

"Huh!? Nothin'!" I quickly slapped closed the notebook and kicked the Colt under the couch and out of sight. "What's up?"

"Want some chicken?"

"Sure."

Somewhere after the second or third piece of chicken and before the first stabs of abdominal pain, Brady asked me about Callahan.

"What's his story, anyway, dude?"

"Hunh, that's exactly what he asked about you. What your story was."

"What'd you say?"

"I told him you were gay."

"What?! What the fuck, dude!" Brady sprang off the couch, sending chicken bones and fried chicken skin chunks flying.

"Hey! Careful, man," I said.

"Jesus fucking Christ!" Brady was spinning in circles, holding his head in his hands. "What . . . thefuck . . . wereyouthinking?"

"What's the problem?"

"Oh, fuck, dude. Dude, fuck!"

"Whatsamatter?"

"Dude, now he's gonna be hittin' on me and shit. Oh, fuck. I'm gonna have ta fuckin' move back to Texas."

"I didn't tell him you were gay. Fuckin' siddown."

"Jesus, dude." Brady fell back onto the couch in relief. "Some shit there's just no joking about. Not with *that* guy. Am I gettin' through to you, dude?"

"You mean Callahan?"

"Yeah, dude. I think your little buddy's gay."

"That's completely possible," I said. "Secretly."

"Well . . . don't you know?"

"I don't know."

"You don't know?"

"It's a secret."

"He's *your* friend."

"Yeah . . . so?"

"So how can you not know?"

"I don't know!" I said. "He *could* be. Look, he *might* be secretly bisexual . . . possibly secretly homosexual."

"Don't you wanna know fersure?"

"Not especially."

"Ya gotta know, dude," Brady insisted.

"And why the fuck is that?"

"Ya just gotta."

"It's a mystery."

"I guess."

"Wrapped in an enigma."

"Shee-iit."

"Stuffed into a puzzle."

"Damn."

We were silent for a moment, pondering the ramifications. Brady looked up at me and said, "Sounds like a job for Homo, P.I., if ya ask me."

"Homo, P.I.? What the fuck is that?"

"A new TV show I'm pitchin' ta Hollywood. Stars Tom Selleck."

"Tom Selleck?"

"You know who that is, don't ya?"

"Yeah. The guy on that show . . . that TV show."

"*Magnum.*" Brady smiled proudly. "*Magnum, P.I.* 'Ceptin' this time . . . he's a homo."

"I'm sure."

"And get this . . . Lookin' for homos. Solvin' homo mysteries like the one your little buddy's got himself mixed up in."

"The kind of guy who can get to the *bottom* of it?" I asked.

"Exactly. Homo, P.I.'s the kind of detective who works on cases of mistaken sexuality."

"A private dick, I take it?"

"You got it, dude. And check this out . . . he drives a Miata."

"Huh?"

"A Miata. Dude, it's only the gayest car ever made. And that assistant of his, the guy with the little homo 'stache? He's also on the show, and he's a homo, too!"

"You are one fucked up person, man."

"What?! Is that so wrong?"

The Party

I parked my wreck of a car across the street from "The House" and turned it off. The Car did its usual two minute sputtering like it might never stop and then finished with a last loud pop and a belch of smoke.

"Dude, you gotta get yourself another car, my brother," Brady stated simply.

"Look, I don't even have a fuckin' job, all right?!" I immediately realized I had barked out this statement as though I suffered from an extreme case of Tourette's syndrome, my mind already drifting back over the shark-infested memories of a tragedy gone by, a wisp of my boyhood asthma resurfacing at the top of my lungs.

"You okay, dude?" Brady asked as he ground out his cigarette.

"Yeah, man, I'm all right."

"Look, we'll just suck up as much beer and free grub as we can and see if we cain't score a coupla cuties."

"Sure," I said with the conviction of an Alcatraz lifer listening to the escape plans of a just-arrived inmate.

"Right in front of her ass, dude," Brady continued. "One of her fuckin' friends!"

"That'd be sweet," I said warming to the fantasy.

"Worse comes to worst, we'll just have to kick her boyfriend's ass. Whassiz name? Rich?"

"Yeah . . . Rich."

Two weeks earlier, Rachel, out of either spite or some sort of misguided gesture of nonexistent friendship, invited me to her place for a barbecue. A very special barbecue. It wasn't even on the weekend. It took place on July 30, a Tuesday. Something about it being Midsummer's Night or something. There was supposed to be an especially good vibe floating about. I think she said magic might be afoot. A time for new beginnings. This suited me just fine because after I accepted the invitation and hung up the phone, I convinced myself that once and for all I would convince myself once and for all that I was through with Rachel. Once and for all.

As we walked up to the house, I heard music drifting out of the backyard and smelled the burning charcoal and suddenly I was feeling pretty good. I really hadn't thought much about Rachel lately. (My feelings after the breakup had evolved considerably. At first, I thought about her constantly, obsessing, some might call it. This was followed by contemplation of stalking her and the like. Then there were the regular private Cottage A weepfests backed by the growing conviction that I would die alone. Soon this became utterly boring, and I realized that while I supposedly missed her, for the life of me, I couldn't really remember what the hell she looked like without the aid of a crumpled, tear-stained photograph. I could barely register an image of her having once slept at my place. The small pile of clothes she'd leave by the side of the bed before crawling under the sheets. Her hairbrush in the bathroom. Her bag on the table. All the condiments she enjoyed that I'd already removed from the fridge and destroyed long ago. My feelings for Rachel had dissipated into an occasional bout of anger and resentment that she'd wasted my time in the first place. I rarely played out the murder/suicide bit anymore. See how much I've grown?)

I rang the bell as Brady regaled me with one of his stories about a trip to Galveston. Back in the day . . .

". . . So the guy made the mistake of callin' Randy a pussy and the one thing you don't call Randy is a pussy, even if you're just jokin' around and such. Well, Randy goes fuckin' nuts, dude. He just flies over the bonfire and is at that poor bastard's throat and is beatin' on him with all he's got. Just bloodyin' him up something bad, dude. Then he drags him over to the dude's car and starts poundin' his face onto the bumper. Sheeit, I thought he might kill him for a minute, but luckily, he wore himself out before that happened, but then, get this, dude. Remember that movie *Mask* not *The Mask,* but *Mask* . . . ?"

The door opened. It was Rachel.

"Oh, hi, Steve." She smiled. "You made it. That's great." While it seemed friendly, I felt that she said this as though I were a kindergartner who had just completed a very successful nap. "Who's your friend?"

"Oh, this is Brady. Andy Brady. Uh . . . this is Rachel."

"Pleased, I'm sure," Brady nodded and touched the bill of his baseball cap.

I was deeply lost looking at Rachel, yet strangely

detached. She was wearing that gauzy tie-dyed blouse I used to hate. I noticed she was even sporting leg and pit hair and had obviously gone out and bought a nice pair of Birkenstocks for Midsummer's Night and when I caught the brief whiff of patchouli, I knew it was true. She had turned into a hippie!

I kinda knew it was coming. Rachel always had a bit of it in her; I guess it just took the breakup to rapidly accelerate her flower child evolution. My presence must have somehow inhibited the budding of her whole-grained goodness.

As we stepped inside, Rachel introduced us to Rich, her boyfriend.

"Rich, this is Steve, remember I told you about . . . ?"

We nodded at each other. Rich was too Kind Veggie for words. Scraggly beard. Guatemalan shorts. Teva sandals. Grateful Dead T-shirt. Tarahumara cloth wrist bands. His hair was two clicks short of street person, and he was sporting a rather gruesome case of eye crusties that, I guess, doesn't bother hippies. I immediately wanted to run out to the car and get the pistol (which for some reason I now, at times, carried in the glove box) and at gunpoint force him to eat steak tartare.

"Dude, you got some shit in your eyes," Brady said and then turned to Rachel. "So, where's that keg at, sweetheart?"

"Everything's out back. Come on, you can meet the other guests."

"She's kinda hot, dude," Brady whispered to me as we headed toward the back.

"Shut the fuck up," I said.

The scene in the backyard was out of my worst nightmare. Not only was it packed with people I didn't know (the few I did were friends of *Rachel's* who would have nothing to do with me once we broke up), not only was I lost in the wilderness of a party's first act (everyone quiet and cringing in the face of human interaction, the sober fulfillment of the social contract, the conversations contrived), not only did I have the disconcerting feeling that I had somehow walked onto the set of a really bad USA Network movie set in the seventies (the fakey dialogue, the stiff manners, the weak costuming, the bad music), but worst of all, the place was jam-packed with hippies, and if there's one thing that gives me the creeps, it's people who think it's still 1969.

Brady and I headed to the keg as though it were our altar and began sucking down beers when at the stroke of six Rich quieted the already rather quiet and lifeless mob by chiming on some sort of miniature Tibetan cymbal rig.

"Everybody? Everybody? Can I have your attention please?" Rich surveyed the lot of us from atop his perch on the back porch, standing next to some sort of gigantic papier-mâché mask of a guy with beard and glasses. "I want to thank you all for coming, and I would like to ring in this year's Midsummer's Night with a moment of silence for Jerry Garcia."

"You gotta be kidding me, dude," Brady said, pissed off.

"That papier-mâché thing's not supposed to be Jerry Garcia, is it?" I asked. Brady simply looked disgusted.

The entire Birkenstock Army bowed their heads in silence as a guy with a guitar and some hippie chick with a flute who looked like she'd escaped from a Renaissance Faire played "Ripple" and then "Sossity, You're a Woman." It was the first time I'd ever seen someone bust out with a Jethro Tull song unplugged, though I did once hear a Muzak version of "Nights in White Satin" at a Chinese bakery.

After the live show, Rich aimed a remote control toward the stereo, fired up Side 1 of "American Beauty," and announced, "May the celebration begin. The goddess is alive and magic is afoot." A lot of the gentle vegans seemed quite moved by this tribute. People were yelling out, "Jerry. Jerry," in a plaintive manner. Others were choking back tears and comforting one another with kind hugs. I was kinda in the same mood myself because Grateful Dead music always fills me with a free-falling anxiety.

With the playing of the music and the passing around of joints and beer and food, the party moved into its second act. People were loosening up and dividing into their assigned cliques. Romance and sex hung in the air in their perfect crystalline form of mere fantasy. The barbecue was glowing, and Brady lucked into some old Zeppelin and slipped it on the stereo. I decided to mingle.

Armed with a full plastic cup of beer, my first attempt at contact with the aliens was an approach of a group of four good-vibed crystal wielders. Unfortunately, their benign positive energy, like some sort of invisible force field, prevented me from approaching any closer than five feet.

Next I walked toward a gaggle of three hippie chicks and weakly smiled their way. They were discussing something about last month's Goddess Shiva potluck and how Sierra wasn't really completely off the lacto or ovo or maybe both and the fact that one of them may have left behind a pair of Huichol Indian salad tongs. I nodded away like someone who didn't speak English and then became concerned that they were analyzing my "energy" and that what they saw wasn't too good.

Once my Uncomfortability Quotient had reached sufficient levels, I moved on. I headed toward a group that included a cute girl I'd been eyeing since arriving. I knew none of them, yet boldly stepped into their group and grunted a "How's' goin'?"

My hot-collared anxiety seemed to instantly kill their conversation. The girl, in fact, looked at me as though I were the famous neighborhood recently pa- roled sex offender. Utilizing an old party trick of mine, I pretended to recognize someone in the distance and with the enthusiasm that Stanley must have shown Liv- ingston, loudly announced, "Hey! That looks like Johnny. I don't believe it. Will you excuse me?"

I quickly headed back to the safety of my only two friends: Brady and that keg of beer.

Brady, after making one quick circuit around the ratty backyard, never really ventured beyond a three- foot radius from the keg. He constantly had that plastic hose in his hand like he was some astronaut stepping out from the mothership and the tap hose was his life- line. He dispensed beer to the guests as though he had arrived with the keg himself.

"Dude, lemme fill you another cup." Brady stuck his cigarette in his mouth and grabbed my plastic cup. "Hey, this here is Charlotte. She's from goddamned France, dude. And I forget your name, sweetheart . . ."

"Monique?" a girl in clunky seventies wear said, exasperated, and with an overly dramatic roll of her eyes.

Brady turned to me. "What the fuck is goin' on, dude? You never told me she was a damn hippie."

"Something happened, man."

"Well, shit, dude, you were lucky you got out when you did. You might be listenin' to The Dead by now."

"Eatin' tofu."

"Gettin' in touch with your inner child and shit."

"Tryin' not to trip over magic what with it being afoot."

"Exactly."

"Or having really bad eye crusties," I said.

"Yeah, what the fuck is with that, anyway?" Brady shook his head in disgust and turned to the women. "So, tell me, Charlotte, they got hippies in France?"

"Oh, well, I zink zo, but . . . aaah, not lahk zees."

"Thank, god, dude, maybe I should just up and move to France." Brady smiled at Monique, who again rolled her eyes as if the idea of Brady in Paris would just fucking kill all of France.

"Hey what'd ya do with our steaks?" I asked.

"Oh, hell yes! Let's fire those puppies up, dude. Care to join us for some real American barbecue at the Lil Smokey, ladies?" Brady asked.

"Oh, no zank you." Charlotte smiled. She was quite intriguing with her French accent, her Euro-punked, slutty clothes, the fishnet stockings, the chlorinated pink hair cut by a drunken barber. "I muss, ow you zay, prepare fah my eckt."

We didn't know what the fuck she was talking about so we refilled our cups and headed to the barbie armed with our meat. Rachel and Rich were sitting off to the side with an overly mellow, possibly albino vegan named, of all things, Cloud.

"You guys having a good time?" Rachel asked.

"Yeah, it's cool. I'm glad I came," I lied technically.

"We're gonna do some cookin'!" Brady grinned devilishly as he tore the gigantic steaks out of their plastic wrapping. The jaws of the vegans dropped at the sight of the impossibly huge, blood-dripping T-bones. "Tain't really a barbecue without a little beef, I always say."

Brady slapped the steaks onto the grill, the juicy fat cap of one nestled and sizzled right up against a tofu weenie that sputtered lamely above the broiling mesquite.

"Careful of my eggplant," Cloud warned. "I still have to marinate it."

Brady took a long hit off his cigarette and shot Cloud a look like either the word "eggplant" or the word "marinate" was a serious insult back in his neck of the woods. Cloud quietly turned away and grabbed a hummus-dipped carrot stick from the picnic table as solace.

I knew we had now crossed the line. The steaks had been the final straw, but the innate mellowness of the vegans left them powerless in the face of the beefeaters as we stood huddled around the fire, marveling at our meat.

Brady and I, swigging beers as though a meteor were hurtling toward Berkeley, leering at the womenfolk, smoking cigarettes, slapping meat on the grill, we came across like a couple of brownshirts crashing a bar mitzvah.

The problem was that when it came to the feelgoody, good feelings of the positive energy crew, the thing they hated more than anything else, more than the Republican Party, more than Japanese whalers, more than CIA operatives or the Guatemalan government, the thing they hated the most were crude, sarcastic, meat-eaters. Especially when we're having a good time, gnawing on some animal flesh.

In my mildly drunken state, I eyed Rachel with a delicious detachment. Her reproachful stares at Brady, her lame-assed tie-dyes, her stupid shit Birkenstocks. What the hell was I ever thinking? That was never going to work. Never. At that moment I felt a wave of freedom and lightness wash over me like the cool breeze that was drifting in from the Pacific.

The bad feelings over the steak and eggplant clash clued me into the fact that we were entering Stage Three of the party. The sun had sunk behind the houses, and the sky had deepened to a breathtaking indigo. I'm not sure if magic was afoot or not, but we'd definitely approached the hour when lone partyers might be found in a corner of the master bedroom weeping quietly, when the bright day's lust and romance-fueled fantasies had been burst, when the first guy gets pushed backward over the near-empty keg, when the next door neighbor bellows from her back porch about how late it is and what little problem she has in calling the police.

At one point through some cruel trick of the Fates, I ended up in the living room in a conversation with Rich, Rachel, and Cloud. Brady was rummaging through the music collection when Rachel asked the dreaded question.

"So, what have you been up to lately, Steve?"

Shit, besides my occasional fantasies of Postal Nightmare Mayhem, I wasn't up to much of anything and yet to admit as much would have been a moral victory for her. It would have meant that it was *she* who somehow held my life together. That without her I was nothing. I didn't know what to say. I was getting no sex and didn't even have a *bad* job anymore.

"Oh, little bit of this, little bit of that," I began to stammer, imagining my face blushing. "Been doing a little writing . . ."

Cloud, Rachel, and Rich were strewn across the couch like the shipwrecked castaways of some New Age

S.S. *Minnow,* desperately looking in my direction as though scanning the horizon for a ship, hoping the tempeh and tamari would hold out.

"I might be going on a swordfishing trip pretty soon. Soon as the seas calm down a bit," I said with the old salt assurance of Captain Bligh.

"We're all vegetarians." Rachel nodded sadly as though I'd just confessed that pedophilia was what I'd been up to lately.

"Meat is murder," Rich added smugly, instantly moving himself up about six places in my Enemies of the Realm list.

"Fuck that shit," came the reply from Professor Brady who was now smoking cigarettes like he was in some kind of tobacco race. "Lotta people earn their livelihoods in cattle."

"That doesn't make it right," Rachel scolded.

"They're doing some great things with tofu these days." Cloud tried to calm the mob.

Luckily, right then Charlotte stuck her head into the room and announced, "Okay! I am ready whizz mah eckt."

Everyone looked at her like we didn't know what the hell she was talking about. Which we didn't.

"Come on." Charlotte motioned for everyone to come outside. "Eet is now, ow you say? Showtahm."

We all made our way out to the back porch where Charlotte was in the process of performing what looked like some dangerous experiments involving gasoline, juggling pins, and a cigarette lighter.

After much *je ne sais quoi* on Charlotte's part and protests from Rachel and Rich, Charlotte lit the clubs, filled her mouth with gasoline, and started juggling and breathing ten-foot flames from her mouth. Rachel was furious and kept warning Charlotte to stop before something really bad happened, Brady and I howled and applauded with all we had, and then, I guess, something really bad happened.

One minute everything was going well. The juggling and fire breathing was quite spectacular and Brady and I agreed that Charlotte was hella cool, when, in a flash, Brady's baseball cap was aflame, Rachel and Rich were yelling "I told you's" at Charlotte, Cloud was attempting to help Brady out of his flaming headgear, and Brady, not knowing what the hell was going on, shoved Cloud into the makeshift Jerry Garcia papier-mâché head, crushing the Captain Trips likeness, while screaming at the top of his lungs, "I've had just about enough of your fucking tofu, dude."

On the ride home, Brady and I agreed we were glad we'd come.

Job Referral #3

I now hang out in front of the lumber and hardware store with the Latinos in the morning, nervously loitering about like a bunch of roadside rest stop homos looking for action. I'm looking for a day's work from some of the various jacked private contractors who ply their wares in the Berkeley-Oakland Hills.

Callahan gave me the tip. He knew everything. He was the only motherfucker who actually grew up in the damn town. Just hang out in front of the lumberyard, he said.

Today, me and this other guy, Orrey, got picked up by Rick. I've worked a couple of times now for Rick. He pays cash, but he's a bit of a dick, is Rick.

Orrey, I don't know if that's a first name, a last name, or how you spell it, but that's who he said he was. Orrey.

Orrey was huge. He had to sit in the back of Rick's pickup attired in a pair of shorts (which kept hitching up on him due to the monumental chafing of his colos-

sal, mahogany thighs) and a far too small T-shirt pro-
claiming some taqueria in San Francisco's Mission.

Orrey was from the valley. Out Modesto way. His
mama was Mexican and his daddy was the ace of
spades. And, as I was sayin', he was fucking huge. The
only straight line on all of Orrey's personage, after you
climbed those massive thighs, past the innertubesque
midriff, beyond the disturbing fat boy's titties, the missing neck, the uber jowls, was a Marine Corps–issue,
stand-at-attention, square block of thick, black crew cut
that glistened with sweat or an overly enthusiastic application of hair products.

The job that Rick had assigned us today was the
exchanging of every bit of furniture in the blue room
upstairs with the computer nook game room downstairs
in Mrs. Biltmore's huge mansion in Piedmont.

This was my second trip to Mrs. Biltmore's with
Rick the Dick. The first time I had to chain gang my
way through sixty-five feet of driveway with this Oaxacan guy to replace some sort of pipe drainage system
and make it more State of the Art. Mrs. Biltmore was
quite enamored with State of the Art and could afford
it.

As we picked our way through the driveway, the
Oaxacan told me of his land. About tamales and big
trees shading the zocalo. How everything was warmer.
Slower. He made it sound exciting, and I wanted to one
day go there.

But today it was Orrey. He worked slowly and le-
thargically. Hauling his ass up and down the stairs practically killed him. He kept gasping for air and telling
me about the great burritos they have at the taqueria
on his T-shirt. Giant burritos. He would demonstrate
their size using both hands, pat his gigantic stomach,
and then roll his eyes in some sort of rapture.

At one point, through some horrible mishap, I came into actual contact with Orrey's giant gut. It happened when we tried to move the endless sofa downstairs. As I looked at the stretch limo–sized sofa and then at Orrey's stomach, which by now had begun to gurgle and plaintively wail for giant burritos, I didn't see how we could ever get the thing through the door.

"They got it in," Mrs. Biltmore said, her voice rising on "in." Like it was irrefutable logic. Which it was. I'm thinking, Don't fuck with me, you rich old hag. I know where you fucking live now. I'll cap your dry, withered ass without a second thought. So don't fucking push!

The doorway was just microns wide enough for the sofa and left no room for either hand or gut. We started jockeying and jimmying the sofa, tilting and turning it in a hopeless attempt at making it shrink in size.

That's when I hit it. I was reaching for sofa and I hit the soft underbelly of Orrey. I think I even detected some sweat moisture. I only hope I didn't recoil in too obvious a horror. He might be a bit sensitive about his weight, you know. But then that wouldn't really explain his choice of clothes. The shorts and tight T-shirt. He should maybe try some sort of Arab gear. Some kind of flowing kaftan affair.

Either way, touching his stomach kind of put me off for work and, it being Wednesday, I decided to take the rest of the week off.

The Evil Dad

I once imagined unemployment as some great vacation, a great opportunity. A chance to realize my potential, to figure out my place in the great scheme of things, but after a couple of months; after hearing Mrs. Park's increasingly disturbing accounts regarding the diversion of water (I'd now watched *Chinatown* three times in a sincere effort at getting to know what the fuck she was talking about); after watching oily Carp eating frozen yogurt nonstop while supervising the fitful and somewhat shoddy work being done on the hot tub (the grand Fourth of July opening pushed back to the fifth and then the tenth and now August was looking good); after witnessing Billy's increased paranoia about someone being out to get him (one day it was the Feds, the next those irksome Hunters Point boys); after hearing Brady's latest (and for once probably justified) fear of homosexual aggression coming at him from Callahan, I don't know, I began to suspect that perhaps I had no potential, that maybe there was no place in this world for me. That something really bad was gonna happen.

But I think what was really bugging the shit outta me was the unavoidable and looming visit by my parents.

Luckily, by sheer chance, Brady was out of town for the scheduled visit and, therefore, unable to accidentally blow my cover of leading a slightly normal, productive, and employed life.

After nine weeks, four days, and seventeen times waking up alone and with a splitting hangover, Brady simply decided he had to get some pussy already, and that the most obvious and immediate solution was to drive the 1,864 miles back to San Angelo and go get some that he painted as breathlessly waiting for him since the moment he up and moved to California.

"Oh, yeah, dude," he told me after he finalized the plan. "Good ol' Ruby. She's a little hottie."

"You know a chick named Ruby?" I asked.

"What, is that so strange to you, dude?"

"Nah, I just never heard of anybody outside of the movies named Ruby. Jack Ruby is the only Ruby I ever heard of."

"Yeah, well, maybe this is his fucking granddaughter, dude."

"Ruby Ruby?"

"Yeah."

"Well . . . is it?"

"No, but what if it fuckin' was? What I'm tryin' to get across to you, Mr. Marooned on a Desert Island, is her hotness, not her dang name."

"Whaddaya mean, Mr. Marooned on a Desert Island?"

"Well, that's about how much you been gettin'."

"Okay, Mr. Drive Halfway Across the United

States. You gotta go to entirely different time zones to get laid."

"Is that so wrong?"

"Well, shit . . ."

"Dude, drivin' a thousand miles for some pussy ain't lame. It combines two of my favorite things in life: a road trip and pussy at the end. All those miles drivin' and it's gettin' late and you're gettin' tired. That dang pussy is like a fuckin' pot a gold at the end of the tunnel."

"The rainbow."

"Whatever, dude. A big ol' juicy pot a gold. YEAH!"

It happened some time after the main courses arrived at Papaetto's, an upscale Italian restaurant down near Oakland. Right about when Dad launched into his bizarre and overly loud story about back in the day. Back when he was a Marine at Pendleton and he and his buddies used to roll wetbacks in Oceanside. The story was told with a rare relish that indicated to me this was some type of good old days to Dad. Some high water mark. It was right then that I wished we spoke different languages. Say I still spoke English, but Dad could only speak and understand Serbo-Croat.

Mom sat as she usually did, placid and impassive. Nearly silent. For the last ten years, Mom's vocabulary seemed to be mostly confined to such pronouncements as, "Are you okay?" or "How is everything?" or "The weather's been *so* nice," and her all-purpose, *"That's* nice." The thing about Mom, though, when she said it, you felt she really did think it *was* nice.

Just as Dad got into the details of how they lured the potential migrant worker/beating victim out of the bar (a nearby table of Latinos kept glaring our way throughout this tale, finally asking to be moved), I began to again formulate my theory that I was not actually related to Dad after all (and, therefore, did not have a postal genetic message to kill and would, consequently, have to change the name of the book). There had either been a mix-up at the hospital or . . .

I turned silently to Mom and shot her a knowing glance. I now knew that I wasn't Daddy's bun baking in her oven that summer many seasons past. You sly dog you, I telepathically congratulated her. Who was it, Mom? Next-door neighbor? Someone from the office? Another *mailman*?

Mom looked at me with her usual expression. The one that said, No one's home.

After the meal, I found myself in my least-favorite predicament involving my parents: sitting in the car while Dear Old Dad drove.

Mom sat in the front passenger seat in her usual demure and innocuous way with her ever-present benign smile (it was an almost beatific Buddha smile that she wore).

I sat dazed in the backseat, suffering from the usual pre-fever symptoms that contact with Dear Old Dad always brought on. A fever that never quite materializes, but one that also never leaves me until some twenty-four hours after Dad goes away. Preferably very far away.

Back at Cedar Manor, Dad paced around, looking, as he usually did, exceptionally disgusted. He had that sour look of his. The one that, over the years, had permanently affixed to his face the expression of one whiffing a particularly nasty fart. Mom was somewhat ill at ease and didn't seem to want to sit down. I took this to mean that the level of discarded fast food containers, empty beer bottles, various chunks of unidentifiable matter on the carpet, and general dust count was far too great for any sort of comfort on her part.

She stood for a moment in her usual glazed silence and then began to clear a spot on the far end of the sofa, underneath a pile of old newspapers. She moved the papers aside and then did a bit of sweeping with her hands before gingerly lowering her slight frame onto the saggy, puke-green sofa, mere inches from the giant protruding spring. Dad continued to pace about the room bitterly.

"I mean, Christ!" he spat. I had no idea what had burned his little bean this time: Mom, Traffic, Mexicans, Me, The President, Mom . . . "You'd think they'd do something about that," he whined.

Mom sat quietly in her now-cleaned spot while Dad, quickly switching gears, began an especially virulent diatribe regarding my Life (look at you . . . look at this place . . . what kind of a job? . . . you shoulda . . . can't you ever do anything right? . . . if you're so smart . . . you need to . . . why, when I was . . .) finishing with his favorite rhetorical: "What the hell is wrong with you?! Sweet limpin' Christ!"

While Dad rested a bit, Mom mentioned some cookies she'd baked. They were in the car. And then she brought up The Baby. Mom smiled at me and said, "The baby. It's so nice."

The impending arrival of what now could only be described in my head as "this creature" filled me with the same dread that TV evangelists try to inspire in the masses regarding the Tribulation. I imagined the delivery of a little monster. The Antichrist in a baby postal uniform. It was gonna be *The Omen* all over again.

"You'll have to come down when the baby's born," Mom said as though it were a sedative. "It's going to be a boy."

"If I can get off work . . ." I lied and then felt sad for the unborn, an unexpected kinship to this future Son of a Mailman.

"So, what's this job you have now?" Dear Old Dad asked loudly, accusatorially, and suspiciously.

My skin crawled as the room came crushing down upon me. Dad seemed to swell to near normal size and the air was close.

"Uh, I'm working at this restaurant . . . in San Francisco."

"Well, why the hell didn't we eat THERE?" Dad bellowed as though he were now the lead in an opera.

"I thought you said you were getting a job at a magazine," Mom said as sweet as pie.

"Oh, *that* job . . ." I stalled. "That job, I *thought* about taking . . . but, it just wasn't any good."

"Ohhh," Mom cooed, feeling my pain.

"Jesus H. Christ!" Dad spat. "I told you you should have gone to West Point."

There was now a silence in the room. A silence I knew only too well. Dad seemed to be kicking at something stuck on the carpet. I was getting a severe case of the bends. Finally, Mom told me about the weather in San Diego. It was nice.

Then Dad angrily asked Mom, "Where'dja leave that?"

"Hmmm?" Mom asked.

"The thing!"

"Oh, it's in the trunk where you left it."

"I'm gonna go get it."

Dad stepped outside and if it wasn't for Mom sitting there so sweet on the couch, I think I might have gone to the closet, fished out the Colt, slapped in the clip, and fuckin' capped Dear Old Dad dead as soon as he returned. I imagined it as a solution of sorts.

"What's *with* him?" I asked Mom.

"Oh, you know ... your father," she said as though the title somehow justified him. "Is everything okay up here, Steve?"

"Yeah, Mom. I'm fine."

"You sure?"

"Yeah." I shrugged.

"You're doing okay?"

"Umm ... all right, I guess." I smiled weakly.

"That's nice." She smiled back.

Dear Old Dad returned with a gigantic tin of cookies that Mom had made special.

"I made those chocolate mint ones you like." Mom smiled, completely unaware that my life had reached a point where cookies alone could no longer save me.

Thankfully, they left after what seemed like a million hours. I sat alone in my room, empty and lost. I was beginning to lose my Hope. One visit from Dear Old Dad and I no longer believed in Love. The intoxicating excitement of post-BagelWorks first taste of freedom days, the sweet redhead that night in The City, hangin' and laughin' with Brady, it was all fading away. Not only fading but leaving in its wake a bitter disappointment, a creeping sensation that mine was not the path of Light. Of Happiness. That perhaps only mayhem and disaster awaited me. Failure and loneliness. A soul-crushing monotony of spiritual and economic poverty. It's not that I wanted this, it just seemed inevitable. It was my Fate. My rage and anger had become, somehow, truer emotions. More authentic than those of Hope or Love.

Things just weren't working out. I couldn't take it much longer. I'd always imagined my life as a success, and the idea of it being a lonely failure frightened me. It had to be someone's fault. Borrowing an old trick of

Dear Old Dad's, I required someone to blame. Scape-goats were in order. A terrible price needed to be paid for my unhappiness, and I would be Collector, Judge, and Executioner.

Who would it be? My Enemies of the Realm List was now so huge as to rival the telephone book. How 'bout Rachel? Boring! Her boyfriend, Rich? A waste of a good .45 slug, though the idea of an enthusiastic pistol whipping, turning his face into a bloody pulp in front of her, pleased me greatly. A random Volvo driver? (Unlike the Unabomber, my manifesto will be entitled "Operation Apfelkuchen." It will document the menace to society that is this Swedish pseudo-luxury automobile.) A smug vegan hippie? Yeah! Shorter? Of course. Always. Carp? There'd be people thanking me. Billy even crossed my mind. I had nothing against him, just the satisfaction of tables turned and him on his knees sniveling for pity as I waved the Colt in front of his craggy face. How 'bout Dad? How 'bout Dear Old Dad? How 'bout that? Would that help?

These thoughts would not leave me. They flooded my mind when I least expected it: late at night when it was quiet, or around crowds of people. Someone needed to pay. The Evil Seed grew.

Pool Hall

Callahan, Brady, and I were down at the Town and Country shooting some half-price pool one fine afternoon. Three wrecks with only a job between us (and that consisted of Brady's high-powered position as fry boy at the Chicken Shack).

Callahan was in his usual semiformal attire. Formal in the sense that he had a buttoned-down shirt and dress shoes. Semi in the fact that the shoes were thin-soled and badly scuffed and the shirt sported various small holes and ballpoint pen stains.

But he did bring three fine cigars for us to smoke as we played. Brady turned his nose up at them, but I took mine. Callahan claimed they were seven-dollar cigars, and I'm sure they were. We even lit them up with these special English matches Cal brought. Thin wooden matches that lit with a snap-to that Cal and I enjoyed.

We had our pitcher of beer, we had our money in the jukebox waiting for our tunes to come up, all of us smokin' our tabacky, crackin' billiard balls across a decent green under the bright lamp and Callahan was already beginning to slip into that odd state of incoherence of his. The one where he turns into a cracked thesaurus misusing ten-dollar words for ten-cent sentiments. The one where, in a confused, circuitous route, Cal nearly reveals a Great Truth only to finish with a word that made no sense at all.

Callahan won the last game and broke, sinking a small one. He chalked his cue with an affectation that came so naturally to him that it wasn't even an affectation anymore.

"You know, I can fall asleep like that." Cal snapped his finger and then took aim.

"It takes me a while," I began.

"But I don't go in very deep," Cal explained as he missed his shot and looked away dejectedly. He sat down on a stool, cue down, beer up. "I'm just under the surface."

Callahan demonstrated his sleeping depth with two flat horizontal palms, sliding one just above the other like he was going to pull shit out of thin air or something. "I've been diagnosed as having a rare form of narcoleptic insomnia."

"What the hell is that?" I asked.

"That's the biggest crock a shit I ever heard," Brady said in an overly aggro manner.

"I'm serious." Cal laughed as though Brady was denying the corruptness of elected officials. "I can sleep while still appearing awake."

"What do you mean?" I asked.

"I'll be walking around, but I'm not entirely cognizant."

"Yeah, well, what the hell are you then?" Brady asked.

"Oh, I may be asleep, yet I'll . . . exhibit an import of consciousness while . . . rescinding in a nether region."

"Yeah, whatever. It's your shot, Magic Man." Brady gave me a look like Cal was fucked up and an asshole or idiot to boot. With both of them looking at me, all I could dare was a shrug.

That was the evening when things started to go sour. After around his ninth pint, Callahan turned bitchy, and the game and the conversation became some sort of incoherent tussle. Brady was in one of his argumentative moods and me? Well, two months with no sex just doesn't seem to mellow me out.

At one point when Cal went upstairs to piss, Brady pulled me aside and told me, "Dude, I think he fuckin' winked at me!"

"What?!"

"I'm serious, dude."

"Maybe he was just being funny."

"Well, that's just it. I don't know if he was or not."

"You don't know?" I asked.

"I don't know."

"You don't know?"

"I don't fuckin' know, dude!" Brady wore a look of troubled anger on his face.

That was the thing about Cal's secret bisexuality (possible secret homosexuality): you never quite knew. He was never seen with a woman, but the same could almost be said for me that summer and I wasn't gay. Occasionally, Cal would mention some girlfriend or, more often, some ex-girlfriend, and he'd make a rare remark when a cute girl walked by, but there was never anything behind it. Callahan's heterosexual world came across like the set of an Ed Wood movie.

And now and then he'd slip up. After too many

162

drinks, Cal might say some *guy* was cute, or he'd make a reference to Martha Stewart, or tonight when Brady's thinking Cal winked at him and no one's sure if he's just being funny and then it's not very funny anymore.

Callahan was coming down the stairs when Brady told me, "I'll fuckin' kill him if he tries anything. Your buddy or not."

As Cal walked up, I knew he imagined we were talking about him. He would have imagined we were talking about him even if we hadn't been, but we had, so we were doubly busted.

"What's up, guys?" Callahan did a rare sharp upward flex of his eyebrows followed by his patented I'm-smiling-but-I'm-really-pissed-off smile.

After an ill silence, I said, "Well, I'm getting an It's-It. Anybody want anything?"

"Get me one a them dogs," Brady asked, fumbling through his pockets.

"Come on, D," I said. "You don't want a dog. Remember what happened last time you had a hot dog here? You don't want to go there."

"Gemme a dawg!"

"You want anything, Cal?" I asked.

Callahan simply pursed his lips at me and produced what looked like about a two-pound bar of chocolate from his coat pocket.

"Gemme a dawg!" Brady repeated.

"All right!" I screamed.

We were slamming down our fast food as the pool table took a break. Callahan offered me, but not Brady, a piece of chocolate. It was good German or Swiss chocolate, and by the time I'd finished my It's-It and broke for the next game, Callahan had polished off the entire kilo of it and was flushed and quite agitated.

We played a couple more games, but now a rotten

tension hung over the pool table like a haze of stale cigarette smoke. Brady and Callahan were acting as though the other wasn't there and the two of them were drinking the pitchers of cheap draft like it was their salvation. As Brady became more belligerent, more argumentative, Callahan began using even bigger words (making up a good many of them as far as I could tell) to make even less sense. I just kept thinking, "I gotta get a girlfriend."

At one point, as Brady was loading up the jukebox with more bills, Callahan pulled me aside.

"I think Roy Rogers is gay," Cal informed me.

"What?! No way; he was married to Dale Evans."

"No, no, no, *Brady*. He keeps looking at me weird."

"Come on." I could hardly believe what I was hearing.

"Yeah." Cal said it with a certain sadness in his voice, as though he hoped this revelation would disappoint me greatly.

"You gotta be kidding, right?" I asked, hoping Cal would finally laugh and say, Yeah, it's *me* who's gay.

"No, seriously. Don't say anything, but I bumped into him over at The Yukon last week. He was, like, coming on to me. I mean, I don't mind if he's gay, but . . ."

"Are you serious, Cal?" I asked with a look that I hoped would say, "Tell me your sins, my son."

Cal tilted his head, pushed his glasses up his nose, smoothed back his hair, and, as Brady returned, began chalking up his cue as though he were trying to start a fire.

The Suit

At this moment I am attired in a $500 Italian suit. It was presented to me by my parents. I had graduated from college, a feat Ole Sis had found impossible, and along with the degree, a stereo system, and a dinner at Mr. A's, I received a finely tailored Italian suit.

Graduation Day. My day in the sun. Ole Sis sat jealously fuming off to the sidelines. Dad filled his breast for the last time with pride for his over-the-years acceptably spindly yet academically gifted son. Back then, Dad could still boast in the face of family and friends as he spoke of his boy's GPA. The world was my supposed oyster and so, his, too.

My great potential never shone so bright as upon that June afternoon five years ago as I stood in the sweltering San Diego heat beneath a highly flammable Halloween costume–like black robe and yellow tasseled mortarboard. My name was called and I walked up nervously and received my diploma. The Mantle of Greatness, twenty-three years in the making, all polished and perfect, awaiting only my reception.

Those were the days.

Tonight? I sit on a ratty seat on a Richmond-bound BART train. My lungs fill with that peculiar BART smell. Not quite buslike, yet neither a subway.

I don't know, today seemed to take forever. My mind felt like it was crammed with cotton candy. I was having trouble acquiring the proper combination of chemicals in my brain that I require to fully enjoy myself. Something was still lacking, a missing element to my special recipe of sugars, salt, alcohol, fat, nitrates, nitrites, BHT, THC, caffeine, polyglycerol esters, and pork by-products.

After I rattled about my room for an eternity, I decided I needed a bockwurst from Top Dog, hoping the salt, pork, and nitrates combined with a Coke might do the trick.

I walked to my ATM and *Fuck It,* I decided in a flash. There was cash in that puppy. Cash I was supposed to save and store and dole out over the coming cold-monthed, trying times ahead with the sensibility of a frugal old matron with nine kids. I was becoming some anal-retentive, frenzied squirrel in the dying days of autumn.

Well, fuck that! In a moment of giddy release, damn the torpedoes, it was full steam ahead. I withdrew an amount. "Get Cash" was my command! "Day-to-Day Savings" was my realm. Oh, the choices the machine offered me. From worry-warted, penny-pinched $20 to Boardwalk—$300. A total I'd rarely known, let alone could withdraw.

I struck $100 with breathtaking excitement. The machine, chinkity-chinkity-chinkity-chinkity, spit out the bills and informed me my balance was at $89.96. Could it help me with anything else? Yes. Put more goddamned money in my account!

The need for all that cash? Well, certainly a fine bockwurst from Top Dog was just what the doctor ordered. And so was that sweet, effervescent Coke. And then? Well, I'm heading into The City in an excitable state with a belly full of bockwurst and cola.

I had a plan. Armed with Italian finery and five crisp twenties (well, four, after the bock and soda) I was going to go to a fancy bar. See how the other half lives. One of those places where the drinks are all six dollars. Where the customers all have Careers. The kind of place filled with Men with Money and the beautiful Egg-ready Women who followed cash and power around. I would walk into one of those places and, bedecked in my suit, pass myself off as a well-off . . . I'm not sure what, but I still had the BART ride to work out the details and with the clothes and my five crisp twenties and my tale of economic upward mobility, maybe I'd even seduce some fine lovely in silk stockings and high heels. A real woman. A professional.

The word alone got me hot. I pictured her up in some high-rise downtown building all day long, sweltering in the stuffy heat of the droning office, rubbing her stockinged knees together, chewing on the end of her pen, counting down the moments to 5 P.M. Hard dreaming about long-awaited romance.

That's what I was dreaming of. Something hot and juicy. A woman whose clothes came off in parts. Tight short skirts. Stockings. Well-starched blouses. The release of heat and perfume. A fine lacy bra. Leave on the heels. Just for me. Jesus! Can't this train go any faster?!

Well, needless to say, it never quite went down as planned. As soon as I stepped into this place called Bix, surrounded by all the swells in their fancy clothes, I immediately felt ill at ease. The blood seemed to drain from the upper half of my body as I slowly dissolved into my lone barstool. Occasionally, someone coming up to order a drink would bump into me and we'd exchange a nod and a smile or a quick "sorry." Beyond that, I somehow hung out my "Social Leper" plaque and was once again in business. My sign read, "No Friends, Need Sex."

I felt that all eyes were upon me. They immediately sensed that I was not one of them. They knew from the way I clumsily ordered a six-dollar cocktail, from the way I walked, from the way I looked nervously about the bar, from the way my ass was parked atop my stool. It was as though I were carved out of stone or was one of those animitronic motherfuckers they have in Disneyland, my movements stiff and awkward.

They *knew* I was the beggar in king's clothing, yet my alienation transformed into a sorry social supremacy. I hated these rich bastards and felt like killing some of them. Their entire lot only confirmed for me my own superiority and the special (though as yet unrevealed) and important role I held in the world. I suddenly missed Brady and a can of beer in the Rose Garden.

I headed back on BART, alone. A haggard veteran returned from a war lost. I felt the fool in my expensive clothes. Clothes I couldn't even wear, remembering Dear Old Dad telling me whose shoes I could never fill and that night feeling him right and feeling lost. A loser.

I'd spent my whole life trying *not* to do things. Trying *not* to please Mom, trying *not* to break up with Rachel, trying *not* to have a career, trying *not* to be like Dear Old Dad (and now trying *not* to go postal) and now that *not* a thing was happening in my life, I floated through the days like an astronaut caught out in space, his lifeline to the module cut off, a useless umbilical cord drifting behind him. Like the astronaut, I see the activity going on inside the spaceship, but am unable to do anything except drift about, helplessly buffeted by unseen forces, waiting for the oxygen to slowly run out.

The Evil Date

I'd been growing tired of the full-blown affair I'd been conducting in my head the last four weeks involving Uma Thurman. Oh, I guess I've forgotten to mention that I'd called it off with Christy Turlington.

Yeah, Christy. For a moment, I thought the gods had smiled down upon me, that Fate was about to take me on a stroll up the sunny side of the street, that my life would soon reside on the right side of the tracks, that clichés didn't always come in packets of three. Through some total (yet at the time meaning-laden) stroke of dumb luck, the Employment Development people sent me on yet another discouraging job interview to yet another sorry-assed restaurant, but this time it was for the Up and Down Club! Don't you get it? Do I have to spell *everything* out for you? Fuckin' Christy Turlington owns the damn place. Or, Turly as I found out her friends call her.

I marched down to BART with a smile on my face and the specter of Love filling my heart. I had it all figured out. Oh, sure, I'd be forced to perform some sort of low-life kitchen scullery nonsense: peeling potatoes, washing lettuce, whipping up Army Surplus vats of bleu cheese dressing for the tasty buffalo wings I was sure they served. But one day Christy, tiring of the phonies that surrounded her in the high-priced world of the runway fashion Ubermodel, would see me hard at work. She'd immediately fall for my winsome personality and boyish good looks. Soon I'd be out of the kitchen and on her arm. I would now only arrive at the Up and Down by chauffeured limousine, but remembering my humble roots, I'd occasionally tour the kitchen, encouraging the disheartened prep cooks ("Son, a short time ago I was just like you, bending down on all fours trying to scoop up spilled grease with a spatula, but don't lose Hope. Look at me now." I motion over toward Christy, who eagerly awaits my return. "I'm tearin' that shit up, dude!").

What actually happened was they put me on the fry detail and my first and last night consisted of dropping beer-battered calamari rings into a bubbling cauldron of 1,000-degree oil and quickly ducking away to avoid the blobs of molten batter that instantly flew out of the fryer and right for your fucking face.

My suggestion to maybe *bake* the calamari next time was greeted with less than enthusiasm by the chef, who gave me sixty dollars (and for some reason an eleven-pound frozen Butterball turkey) at the end of the night and told me to forget that I'd ever been there and that he would try and do the same.

Well, that was it for me. I dumped Christy. Cold. No warning. She can fucking cry herself to sleep at night for all I care. It was time for a change.

It was Uma Time. New York City. The bright lights. Me and Uma. We sit around at expensive restaurants laughing and being very witty. Then it's off to bed where Uma's anxious heat far outshines the cool soft comfort I'd found in the impossibly long and perfect arms of Christy. Uma has a great sense of humor, but, more importantly, the most amazing moist mouth the gods have ever dreamt. I find great comfort there and all is right with the world.

But then I wake up and remember the mannequin that caught my eye this morning and realize all is not right with *my* world and I feel a desperation close down upon me. I can barely breathe as the wind is knocked out of my chest and all seems impossible and I wonder on my Fate and why can't anything just work out right? Why can't something good just happen for once?

I guess that's why I let Callahan arrange a blind date. It was getting bad. Not just going out on a blind date, but letting Callahan set it up. He's *never* with a woman (thereby leading me to believe that it's homosexuality that is his possible secret).

But he said he knew this girl. "Remember that girl?" he said. Some sister of a friend or friend of someone's sister, I'm not sure. It wasn't technically a blind date because I'd met her once over at Old Man Callahan's and Callahan the Younger claimed she'd asked about me.

Dana was her name. "The blonde," Cal said, "don't your remember?" I remembered her as rather more attractive than I'm used to. Like a twisted Florence Nightingale, I'm often drawn to the homely girl. It's not rehabilitation I offer, just my own hope of not being rejected. I imagine their homeliness will be my entrance. The wallflowers, the second-best sisters, the Plain Janes. Those are my kind of girls.

I'm not sure if you're aware (I'm fairly certain Dana wasn't), but for some reason, my entire existence revolved around this date. My view of the Universe (Was it cold, hard, and cruel, or a sweet lover's paradise?) and my position within it depended entirely on the outcome of this date.

I wouldn't, of course, tell *her* as much. On the surface hung only the usual weight of tentative first-date anxiety, but in the back of my mind lay the expectation of an entire Life. All hung in such a balance that this young woman held in her bosom my future. It could only be as such.

Dana was unaware of all this as I picked her up at her place and when she opened the door, the first thought in my mind was, *Oh no, not* that *chick. I thought Cal meant the* other *one.* It was the girl I got into the argument over Birkenstocks with and I noticed her face fall as she recognized *me,* the one I seem to remember her referring to as "just a bitter asshole."

As I waited for Dana to put some sort of frantic finishing touches to her night's persona, I eyed the long legs of the mini-skirted, somewhat hotter roomie and began to slip into the depths of despair that accompany the thought that I'd *never* get to fuck someone like *this* girl. But I hung in there and disregarded the usual pessimism Dear Old Dad had planted in my mind and, unusually, hoped for the best.

We were at a restaurant and Dana was almost looking sumptuous in a tight, lime-green short dress she'd somehow wriggled into for our once expectant, now excruciating first (and last) date. I think it was a sort of push-up affair because I didn't remember nearly as much bosom on our first encounter, but there they were, bursting forth like ripe summer fruit.

I'd been having trouble with dating lately. Beyond the usual fact that almost no one will go out with me. I pondered this problem as Dana decided on whether it was the ricotta cheese and spinach ravioli in a lemon cream sauce, the red pepper fettuccini with diced ham in a cream and cheese dairy medley, or the mesquite-grilled Seven Cheese Chicken that she wanted. My problem was that while I would fuck virtually anything that could be declared pre-op female (and probably eagerly fall for many post-op cases), my soul, a somewhat deeper bell, just wasn't being rung. In a word, it all left me cold ultimately, and I knew from word one that Dana was such a case.

"I always wondered, why did they call themselves The Police?" Dana asked as though she were revealing a serious discrepancy in the Warren Report. "Why would they call themselves The Police, ya know?" She nodded knowingly.

Oh, my god, I thought. What is she talking about? Obviously the heavy and repeated application of mousse has affected her mental health. How does she get her hair to stand so high? I must make a note: No more going out with women with Big Hair.

"Yeah, that is kinda funny," I managed.

"Isn't it?" A bit flushed from the wine, Dana touched my forearm as though we were now soulmates based on our bonding over something involving Sting, the Birkenstock Affair long forgiven. *I hate Sting!* I'm thinking and tell myself sternly, *Concentrate on those breasts.*

"Well, huiuuck!!" I coughed. "Hrraaackch!" I'd sucked up a baby lettuce leaf into the lower depths of my lungs. It being a first date, I tried to pretend that nothing had happened, tried to bring up Sting's decent performance in *Dune,* but this was complicated by the fact that I was unable to get any oxygen. I tried one more deep, strong sure cough from the bowels of my soul and, luckily, expelled the troublesome green. Unfortunately, it flew across the table and pasted itself on Dana's wineglass. She shot me a look that seemed to say I had confirmed for her, at last, that all men *are* scum.

• • •

2:45 A.M. It was just a girl. Just a girl I wanted. I ached for it. I was starved for a soft, gentle touch. Dana, fuck Dana. The only thing that could save me was Love. For a time, merely longed-for, sweet, imagined Love was enough. That cocktail girl at The Yukon. The girl at the café. That one I saw one bright morning on the street. The one I would never again see for the remainder of my life.

I dreamt hard and satisfyingly of her. That pretty face. It's always the face that haunts me the longest. Only the face steals my heart away. From their eyes and their dazzling smile I imagine them sweet as can be. I imagine redemption. I imagine the mornings waking so content and warm under the covers of last night's Love. It's just a girl. Just a girl I want.

And not just *any* girl. *The* girl. The girl I want. She'd love me right and never lie and never leave and in her I'll find myself. In her eyes I'll see the possibilities of perfection. In her arms I'll know the comfort of devotion. At her breast I'll breathe the very breath of grace. Love.

But not tonight. Tonight, Cottage A sits deathly quiet as Berkeley sleeps, as the entire West Coast from Seattle down to fucking Dago snuggles comfortably under their warm and happy covers. After the disaster of tonight's date, I've become a bit unglued. I have the headphones on, blaring at probably eardrum-damaging volumes. Bob the Cat sleeps the deepest, most profound sleep at the foot of the bed, unaware of the mayhem I have planned as I polish the Colt .45 Gold Cup, a full clip of the now-banned Talon cartridges on the nightstand. The Chronic is playing and Dr. Dre is exhorting me to "break 'em off." I stare straight ahead, unblinking, as though in a trance. A disbeliever with a clear message. Destiny has me by the balls again.

| Morning

My eyes snap open to the deadening reality of yet another same old day. I toss aside my JC Penney pale blue floral print cottony-flannelly sheets and check the time on my $5.99 Equity mini-alarm. It's a lightweight black plastic clock with a knob in the back that adjusts both the time *and* the alarm setting. Duct tape holds the two AA batteries in place. It's 7:35. It's always 7:35.

I pull on a pair of faded, knee-shredded Levi 501s, 32 waist, 34 length, and slip on a pair of Gold-Toe socks (three pairs for $7.99), which might now be more accurately described as "Black-Heeled."

The shirt I've chosen for today is what is commonly known as a "tee." Specifically, it's a Beefy-Tee by Hanes, is black, and features a leering photo of Charlie Manson. The sleeves are cut high on the biceps and, tucked in, the T-shirt accents a lean waist and well-developed pecs (unfortunately, of the three muscle groups mentioned, I only possess the lean waist).

176

My shoes are black lace-up ankle boots by Dexter (a Christmas gift from three years back). They're badly scuffed, and the soles are thinning, but they've got at least a couple more months before I need to use the ever-versatile duct tape on them.

I head the ten feet into my "living room" and turn on my Realistic combo receiver/tuner/CD player to Howard Stern. Today he has on one of my favorites, a porno chick. He's asking if he can grab her ass and squirt whipped cream on her. "Oh, what I'd do with you . . ." Howard says.

I then head into the kitchen for a slug of Evian (actually tap water in an Evian bottle) and some toast. I place two thick slices of Acme Pain au Levain into my Proctor-Silex toaster. It's the model with both a lever for lowering the bread into the twin toast slots up top *and* one to adjust the darkness, ranging all the way from "light" to "dark."

As the toast burns, I head into the bathroom to piss and then wash up at my American Standard porcelain sink that sports a yellowish patina of grime, whiskers, and hair. I dry my face with a terry towel by Cannon, a pale purple one that no longer worked in Mom's color-coordinated bathroom.

Back in the kitchen, I'm scraping the carbon off my Pain au Levain as I boil some water for a cup of Peet's Viennese Blend coffee. My plastic Filtropa filter holder (imported all the way from Holland) fits nicely over my Sea World coffee mug that sports a picture of a diving Shamu. I then realize that, again, I'm completely out of Melitta's No. 2, nonbleached, dioxin-free filters, and I am forced to use a paper towel. It's a high-quality, superabsorbant design by Brawny. This little misfortune with the filters nearly reduces me to tears and almost crushes my spirit for the entire day.

I sit on my puke green sofa (unknown make, requistioned off a street corner in Piedmont before the Salvation Army could get their greedy hands on it), drinking my coffee, eating my toast, and crushing ants on the wobbly coffee table. The table is littered with Chicken Shack boxes full of bones and empty mashed potato containers, the Colt (which I'd been doing a little role playing with the night before), and a couple of aluminum faux ashtrays Brady used (actually beer cans by Tecate).

This morning I'm too lazy to use my favorite method on the ants—boiling water—and crush them individually with my index finger. Their collective consciousness soon alerts the entire group as they scurry about frantically. Despite my ceaseless war against the ants, I never kill spiders in my house. Quickly bored, I finish my coffee, head out the door, and hope that something will happen to my life today.

Bowling in Napa

It all began as a beautiful sunny summer morning. Around eleven. The sun was up and all warmed up and Brady and I were sitting on the Manor lawn in our folding lawn chairs. I had slammed back enough coffee to momentarily hold the Evil Seed at bay. We were eating toasted bagels (see, I'm getting over the 'Works now) and some plums Mrs. Park brought by with a nervous smile and a half-hearted comment about checking the back. August was a hard time for Mrs. Park for the weather was as hot and dry as it got in these parts and water was hard to be found and the conspiracy of Carp's Hot Tub Water Diversion became a test of faith.

With us also was Cara. Brady's new "chick" as he referred to her. They'd been going out a coupla weeks and by now I'd gotten over the initial disappointment at having my buddy getting laid (I really don't like to think *anybody* I actually know *ever* has any actual sex if I'm not getting any) and Cara even promised to set me up with one of her less fucked up and embittered friends.

The plan was to head up to Napa and hit all the wineries for free samples. Brady had it dreamed up like he'd just be staggering from winery to winery with his commemorative wine goblet in hand. I tried to tell him it didn't work like that anymore. That you either had to pay for the shit or go on some ridiculously endless tour of the works for your three glasses, one ounce each, of three different pedigreed wines. It was a lousy way to tie on a cheap drunk, but he just wouldn't listen.

Somehow, Brady had obtained the use of Billy's prized GTO that afternoon and we were soon powering up the freeway to the Napa Valley.

"Dude, someday I'm gonna get me a car like this baby." Brady was as happy as could be behind the wheel. "Ya know, Billy said maybe he'd sell me this one."

"No way," I said. "How much?"

"Thirty-five hundred dollars, I think."

"Thirty-five hundred dollars?!"

"Dude, it's cherry."

"Where are you ever gonna get thirty-five hundred dollars?" Cara asked.

"Shut the fuck up! I could."

"Where? At the Chicken Shack?"

Brady knitted his brow. "I seen you nibblin' on some extra crispy wings, motherfucker."

"So?"

"Lookin' like some little squirrel gnawin' away."

"Least I get it before it turns green." Cara turned to me in the backseat. "Get this, I seen him peel moldy skin off and eat it. He don't even care."

"Bullshit! I get it fresher than anybody here. I'm at the muthafuckin' source, dude, so fuck you!"

"Fuck you!" she said.

I slipped back. I slipped behind my shades. I slipped into the comfort of the plush leather seats and watched the countryside slide by as the lovebirds attempted to bitch slap each other while going seventy.

I began to kick at some of the crap Billy had left on the floor of the back (*Outlaw Biker* magazines from the Carter Administration. A hundred-year-old PBJ sandwich that appeared to have once molded badly and then dried into a cow-pattylike wafer thing. Various tools for either some serious on-the-road car repairs or some serious street fighting: socket wrenches, three-foot lengths of metal pipe, chains, medieval farm implements). I popped open the ashtray and found a very dry, rather large roach that Billy must have forgotten in some other decade.

"Hey, look what I found!" I held up the roach like a proud, successful hunter. They didn't hear a thing. An argument over some radio song had resulted in the two of them looking sullen and miserable in the front seat. Oh, true love. I can barely wait for my own.

No matter. I broke out some matches. Let's see what visions Billy has left for me in this fine old mid-sixties Detroit powermobile. Listen to that engine rumble. The vibration has given me a throbbing hard-on. My cock's about to burst through at a spot where the sun is baking my pants leg. It's like an oak seedling struggling to sprout.

Hmm, so perfumey. Definitely not Northern Californian sinsemilla. I exhaled and took another long hit and then a third.

"Hey, dude! What the fuck you got there?" Brady caught my eye in the rearview.

"Want some?" I offered.

"Yeah, gimme that!"

I exhaled slowly, dreamily, and watched as the smoke was sucked out the window in a flash. As I melted into the seat, I began to marvel at the beautiful California countryside racing by the window. Rolling hills studded with oaks. Green fields of grass long since turned their summer tan. Pines lined the tops of the mountains that lie along both sides of the valley. The air was fresh and real. And I felt the heat of the sun as we left the cool moist realm of The Bay in the rocketing coach of Pontiac's 1967 GTO.

I fell into the happiest of reveries back there. Something with maidens aplenty and agrarian-based economies. Perhaps an occasional barroom fight with broadswords. The goblets overflowed with wine made from all those grapes sitting out there on the endless summer plain. There was a young woman by my side and I had my sleeves rolled up and the wind blew through my hair as the sweat beaded upon my sunny brow from a good day's work.

But then . . . I don't know. I couldn't imagine my job. What was *my* task? How did I fit in? Ah, it was fake. Suddenly my fantasy turned black. It seemed too much like a Renaissance Faire, and I hate those! And then I had this nervous moment where my breath caught high up in my lungs, almost in my throat, and I'm thinking, this car is going way too slow. We're going way too slow! AND THE OTHER CARS! THEY SEEM WAY TOO SMALL!! Billy has put something in this roach. Oh man, I'm fucking on some Hells Angels PCP Death Trip circa 1974, man!

I wanted to ask Brady what the fuck was going on, but was having a little trouble speaking. That's when I noticed we were pulling into a strip mall. One of those minimalls! We're suddenly somehow back in San Diego and now I'm on the lookout for mailmen! And the gun's at home. Sweet limpin' Christ!

"We ain't in San Diego, dude," Brady told me as he pulled into a parking slot and turned off the car.

"What the fuck is he talking about?" Cara asked half pissed off and half concerned. "You got some freaky friends."

"Dude, come on, dude," Brady said. "We're going bowling."

"Huh?" I asked. Brady simply nodded his head. "Bowling?"

"That's right," Brady said.

"What about the wine?"

Brady shook his head. "Bowling. Let's go."

Bowling sounded good right then.

With Brady definitely and myself possibly in the formative years of severe alcoholism, we first stopped off at this cheesy little bar they had inside the bowling alley.

"Oh, dude! This is a sweet bowling alley." Brady beamed. "Jus' loogithat, they even got a little diner in here. Yeah!"

"I can't believe we're in a bowling alley," Cara complained. "That is *so* lame. What about the wineries?"

I was still trying to get a grip on the effects of Billy's hidden roach and was yet to be convinced that I hadn't inhaled into my lungs some Pandora's box of hellish visions and permanant health damage.

Complicating matters was the realization that while we *weren't* in San Diego, we did now appear to be quite a bit closer to Brady's hometown. There were button-down gingham shirts all over the place, guys in cowboy hats and boots, and women with feathered hair. It was a Caliornia shitkicker's fest. We grabbed a booth in the lounge.

"I'm tellin' you, dude, they're dwarves."

"No way!" I argued with Brady.

Cara nodded her head and looked at me pleadingly. "Dwarves."

"Just look, dude," Brady said.

I squinted my eyes and in the darkness of the bar, through my vastly altered and somewhat disturbing perception from smoking The Curse of Billy's Hidden Roach, I attempted to determine if the two gentlemen sitting at the bar were, indeed, dwarves.

I was so deep in thought looking at the one in the nice red dress shirt that I didn't notice that his partner, wearing a tight tank top, had walked over to me (turning out to be an actual dwarf), reached up to my shoulder and gave me an angry shove.

"What are you looking at?" he asked angrily.

I was caught red-faced and -handed and as I watched him clench his tiny hands into tiny fists, I realized that this little person was ready to scrap! And if we did, even if I mopped the place up with his lilliputian ass, people would say, "He only beat a dwarf. Pick on somebody your own size!" But looking at his ripped arms, his miniature massive chest (he really was, what with the beard and all, a three-and-a-half-foot-tall Hercules) I came to the conclusion that this guy could probably lay a whippin' on me.

(Right then The Evil of Billy's Hidden Roach sent an image into my brain of the little guy flying off the floor and wrapping himself around my chest region, pummeling away at my head like some mental patient.)

I looked him hard in the eye. "I was just wondering if you guys wanted to do some bowling with us."

"Oh." The little person smiled and wrung his wee hands. "Wanna lay some money on it?"

We were down by twenty-four pins with three frames to go.

"Come on, Stevie boy," Brady cheered me on. "Lay a hurtin' on them pins."

I hadn't bowled in years (my score, which hovered in the high eighties, attested to this), but was developing a bit of a form and began to feel comfortable in my strap-on bowling shoes. I took careful aim, clumsy-stepped to the line, and slid the ball down the lane.

Crack! The pins exploded in all directions. A strike!

"Dude, yeah! Yeah, dude!" Brady howled.

" 'At's right." I strutted back to the plastic seats. "A couple more Budweisers and I'm joining the league, dude."

As Earl, the ripped dwarf in the tank top, effortlessly hoisted his sixteen-pound ball and began his six hundred-step approach to his silent release, my eyes again wandered about the alley.

It was a weird mix of people who appeared to have been bused in from Oklahoma trailer parks along with fresh-faced farm boy types squiring the most beautiful junior high school girls I've ever seen. By the fifth frame, I'd been transformed into a drooling Humbert Humbert in red-and-tan bowling shoes. These girls, especially the cocoa-skinned Latinas with long, black hair and infinite coal black eyes, were too much. I'd have had my usual rush of lust followed by the heart stabbed feeling that they'd never be mine except for their youth. These were *girls*. Innocent and pure, wearing their fresh milk smiles, still with teddy bears and toys. Too young to be toyed with by the likes of me.

There was one couple in particular. He was scrubbed cheeked as he seriously aimed his ball in the clumsy, cocky bravado of the adolescent. His girl was tender beauty ripening before my eyes. Big white teeth marked her broad smile. Her dark almond eyes seemed connected to the earth, bearing a faith I might never know.

I loved that couple. I loved their nervous eager love. I loved the mixing of their far-apart genes. She came from a thousand miles to the south, maybe three. And him, his family might have been one of those that came to America in a wooden boat—red-haired and freckled.

"God, I love America, sometimes," I said to Brady, wistful and serious.

"Yeah, dude. It's a sweet old country." He nodded and drifted away for a second. "But fucked up, too. Really fucked up."

"I know it. No denying, but there's something about the land. Something special. There's just gotta be."

"Sure. Looks like I'm up." Brady grabbed his ball and tugged at his goatee as he sometimes would. Earl took the seat next to me.

"You know, you guys are really cool," I said.

"You mean for little people?" He looked serious for a second and then laughed.

"No, no. For anybody, man. You guys are all right."

The great thing about the little people, besides them being generally nice guys, was that I didn't feel like Brady, Cara, and I were such obvious freaks anymore. When we first walked in, I felt all eyes upon us. I might have blended in, but not Brady with his long hair, goatee, and tattooed forearms. And Cara, she was wearing some outfit with extreme platform shoes from some obscure corner of the seventies disco era, not to mention her pierced face combo that looked like she might have been caught at the sewing supply stand at the flea market during hurricane force winds.

But the little people didn't care about all of that. We accepted them for who they were, and they accepted us for who we were and gladly took our forty dollars after they won and then even offered to buy a round of drinks.

Billy Bud

I got this bud from Billy. Mendo buds. He assured me they were of the finest quality. He was right. I haven't left my cottage since I split an eighth with Brady four days ago. Supplies are running low. I'm down to my last three-quarter pound can of Dinty Moore and a single can of Veg-All. The pound-and-a-quarter bag of Oreos were gone by nightfall of the first day. I've been reduced to boiling down the remains of a box of sugar with some water to create a sort of homemade cara-mel—a trick I learned at that one restaurant job. I'm administering myself tablespoons of this mixture on the half hour. If the weed doesn't run out soon, I may starve to death.

Worst of all, I haven't read a paper since becoming housebound on Monday. Things became so desperate that on Day Three, I broke down and read Herb Caen's column from Monday's tattered old news. You see, I *need* the tragedy of others. I *need* to know about the homeless people frozen solid each winter in Chicago

(Bumsicles Billy gleefully called them as he slapped me on the back and popped open a sixteen-ounce can of Bud). I *want* to know about the slaughter in Africa. I'm *fascinated* by the three hundred bodies an hour floating down that river in Rwanda. I'm *stunned* by the hole in the sky.

AIDS, rivers catching fire in Eastern Europe, children nailed to telephone poles in Bosnia. I become almost giddy with the slaughterhouse numbers: double the people in forty years; four thousand acres of rain forest cleared daily; viruses that no antibiotic can kill becoming commonplace in five years. It's all quite breathtaking.

I remember Grampa on Mom's side when he came and visited. He'd sit out on the back patio, with his old guy suspenders, his hand atop a gnarled wooden cane, and he'd tell me in his thick smoky voice about how much better it was in the old days. About how the world was going to Hell. I figured old guys have been telling that one since they *had* old guys, since there *were* "the good old days."

The way Grampa told it seemed almost charming, so far off and faded. It was like he was running one of those flickering old newsreels past me and while the tale was supposed to be alarming, it merely came off as quaint and mildly amusing. I imagined it an almost out-of-date tradition: Old Man tells Youth about how World has gone to shit. Youth, confident and eager, remains unshaken in the conviction that they will make the World an even better place.

Unh-unh. Not anymore. I don't even have to wait for my hair to turn white and the canes to be passed out to lament a time gone by. The World falling apart no longer takes a man's lifetime. It has the immediacy of a car wreck happening before your very eyes, with *you* behind the wheel and no way to avoid the impact.

And where might I possibly fit in such a world? *Hard Copy* comes to mind. I wonder if they'll pick up on the subtleties? Will they lead with, "The *son* of a postal worker went on a murderous rampage today . . . ?"

"He was described by neighbors as a quiet, polite young man . . . he'd recently lost his job and his girlfriend left him for a hippie . . . authorities could find no real motive for the killings, but a rambling manuscript found on the killer titled "Enemies of the Realm" mentioned Fate, Destiny, and an Evil Seed of Postal Hate . . . his father, in a paid-for-in-advance, exclusive *Hard Copy* interview said, 'Sweet Limpin' Christ! I told him he shoulda gone to West Point. Thank God I took that life insurance policy out on him.' . . . the killer's mother, sobbing uncontrollably, only issued this statement: 'He was so nice.' "

It would be *something* at least. At least I would gain *some* measure of fame and notoriety. My world, as it now stood, was nothing. I had nothing. My love was lost and sat within my chest a painful, excruciating cancer. My future lay before me a troubling and frightening blank, seemingly hopeless. The world itself, the planet, was a horror on a scale I could hardly conceive. Everything was *so* fucked up. My life seemed *so* fucked up. *So* lonely. Why not? Why not just fucking go off?

To Blood Bank or
Not to Blood Bank

I am again contemplating a run down to the blood bank for some quick cash. Not only will I receive eight dollars, a cookie, and a glass of orange juice, but they throw in a free AIDS test to boot. I *have* considered trying the sperm bank. Not only would my masturbation then be subsidized, but I could help out in the creation of a Master Race. Unfortunately, being unemployed makes my seed somewhat less desirable. I'm stuck with blood and plasma.

The problem is that a visit to the blood bank is *so* pathetic. It makes going to the Employment Development Department look like a visit to the White House. Selling your bodily fluids is nothing to be proud of. If my old man saw me in line at the blood bank, he'd have a shit fit, but he still wouldn't float me a fucking dime. Thinks that would fuck me up, sap my initiative. Wrong! What's fucking me up is sitting at home wondering if it's worth trading a couple of hours and some blood for enough money to buy a regular burrito and

191

a cheap sixer of beer (not to mention the cookies and juice). It's decisions like *that* that are fucking me up.

After a bit, I decided I wasn't in the right state of mind to have my bodily fluids tampered with. My mental state has become something of a biohazard and should only be approached if you are completely encased in a full-body suit of nonpermeable wonder polymer/latex materials. My moods are tender and changeable. I'm something of an emotional chameleon. Cup of coffee: Life is a paradise and I am its King, but seventeen minutes after slamming down three chocolate raised donuts? Life is no longer worth living. I hear a good song on the radio and I am filled with fire and brimstone. The latest song by the Stones and the world becomes a phony sham. The sweet soulful words of Kerouac and I swell with inspiration and determination. One flash of *Friends* on the TV and I'm filled with a near-uncontrollable murderous rage.

Rachel used to say I should take Prozac, but my system can only tolerate illegal substances. A hot glass of Theraflu sends me into hyperagitation backed with violent imagery. What would Prozac do, especially given the mailman's blood that courses through me?

My latest funk began last night when I made the grave mistake of buying some newfangled fudge cookie instead of staying with my true love: Oreos.

At Safeway there seemed to be some sort of jam-up at the cookie/cracker/jelly aisle. I think there might have been a wreck in front of the new half-fat Oreos. It was a fucking frenzy! People were crowded four deep in front of the cookies. Supplies were running low. Shoppers were beginning to hoard. They stacked Keeblers, jammed their carts full of Flakey Flix, loaded up on the overpriced LUs. It was getting down to the

Teddy Grahams, man! But I couldn't get through. My only chance was to get around to the other side before it was too late!

I zipped up the other aisle, and it was clear sailing past the cereals. I threw in a box of Froot Loops just in case the cookies proved impossible. Now I was set. Armed with the Froot Loops, it was all gravy from there, and in the excitement, I quickened my fast walk back to the cookies.

I don't know what it is, it's not like I'm a fat fuck, but I always feel self-conscious as I hit the cookie section of my friendly local neighborhood supermarket. It's the same thing at the magazine section of the bookstore. When I pass *Penthouse* and *Playboy*, I'll shoot the sidelong glance, manage an imperceptible slow-down. Oh my, naked women with goddess bodies airbrushed to further perfection? Juiced up for my consumption? Perhaps I'll take a look, but no! A four-foot-tall, white-haired lady is now behind me, eyeing me disapprovingly. I reach instead for *U.S. News and World Report*. Let's examine Sri Lanka's trade deficit. Hand me that *Zyzzva,* I want to enjoy sub-Commandante Marcos's latest poetry.

It's the same with cookies. I pretend to study the nutritional information on a bag of fat-free Fig Newtons, but secretly I'm staring at a package of cookies decorated with happy elfin fudge people dancing merrily. I quickly stashed the fudge elfs into my hand basket and placed a head of lettuce on top for camouflage.

Then it was off to the canned goods. It's one of my favorites. Good old canned goods. Again I found an opening and was working my way through the shoppers like Emmitt Smith. I'm picking up steam, carts are moving out of my way, I'm bobbing and weaving, the tiny white-haired lady backs away with a dirty, worried look. Boom! I hit the Campbell's soup section, and I'm on top of the world.

A coupla Hungry Mans, some Dinty, and some hash. I got my beer, I got my cookies, the head of lettuce so I don't look like I'm slumming too bad when I hit the checkout line (I hope it's not that one lady, the one that reminds me of Mom. I can almost hear her sigh in disappointment as she scans my USDA Minimum Requirement–deficient purchases).

As I grabbed a can of Veg-All, a particularly attractive display of canned peas caught my eye. Now I needed *peas*. Badly. Then I remembered those peas Mom used to make seven or eight times a year. Always on Thanksgiving and always on Easter. The tiny peas. Petit pois. They were French. Leseuer, monsieur. Sweeter, more tender. Trés magnifique! How I loved them.

However, instead of just loading a couple of the silver cans into my basket, I began to channel Dear Old Dad and attempted to mentally work out the price of the myriad peas, get a basic peas-for-the-penny estimate. I now needed to know whether I had to stay in the Townhouse midlevel pea range (still thumbing my nose at the generic can of peas that states simply and boldly—but remains somehow untrustworthy—that it is indeed peas and nothing more, nothing less) or could I throw caution to the wind, unemployed as I was, and dine tonight on fancy baby peas?

But that night I was a wild man. Fuck caution! Fuck my old man trying to save pennies. I loaded two cans of Leseuer peas into my cart and wondered, Would the Green Giant really don a beret to hawk peas? I always pictured him as somewhat parochial and perhaps a bit of an isolationist.

As I approached the checkout line, I noticed this

cute girl I'd been eyeing over in the cheese section. A sweet young thing in a soft wooly black top, short skirt, and those black stockings I love, oh, so much. A little Latina with café con leche skin and thick, luxurious hair. As I began to unload my basket, she actually spoke to me, and within seconds of our nonsense conversation, I'm imagining love, lust, infatuation, marriage, and children, bending her over and taking her from behind. Then she mentions that the cookies I'm purchasing are her boyfriend's favorite cookies. Her boyfriend? FUCK HIM! Who the fuck said anything about boyfriends, anyway? Smile at me while you got a boyfriend waiting for cookies at home, eh? We'll just see about that.

I walked home miserable. Reality was crashing down upon me. Simple sweet fantasy, a pretty girl's alluring smile, a short exchange, the meeting of eyes, back in July, this alone was simply enough. A few short weeks ago, my mind could float away on fantasy's magic carpet ride, blissful and unaware. Now, in the depths of the Bay Area's lacking August heat fantasy was a tattered old curtain no longer up to the task of shielding me from reality's blistering, unflattering light. The only fantasies that carried any weight these days involved murder, mayhem, mailmen, and the Mark IV.

But the day wasn't a total waste. I did determine, at last, that it *is* possible to shop at Safeway with a fully loaded semiautomatic pistol tucked into your coat pocket. No one seems to notice or care.

Ole Sis Again

Ole Sis called again today. Shouldn't there be a rule about phone calls? How about this one: when you call you've fucking got *something* to say? That seems like a good rule.

I must admit, though, that from the start, Ole Sis said she only called to see how I was doing, that Mom was worried about me. I don't really remember the call exactly. Ole Sis caught me at a bad time.

In one of my increasingly frequent moments of alone-in-my-cottage insanity, I had, just prior to the phone call, been doing a bit of playacting involving a faded purple overcoat, my postal worker shirt, and the Colt .45.

I was modeling the latest in this fall's psychowear in front of my full-length mirror (well, full-length if you rode horses at Bay Meadows or were Dear Old Dad's size). My hands were buried deep into the ample pockets of the overcoat, my right hand gripping the pistol. I flipped up the collar. I felt my look could be described as "bad," perhaps even "fly."

I began to pace back and forth in my trashed living room, kicking aside piles of Chicken Shack boxes filled with gnawed chicken bones, wadded-up clean-wipes, and tiny clear plastic containers coated with the remnants of congealed Chicken Shack gravy.

I looked at the mirror each time I walked past. Left, right. Back and forth.

"Hey, G," I said to the reflection, " 'sup? Huh? Huh? I'm standing here. You make the move. You make the move. It's your move."

I whipped the pistol out and pointed it at my reflection. "You want a piece a me, Shorter? Huh? Bagel boy? How 'bout you, Carp? Volvo bitch. What'd you say about rent? I'm sorry, I didn't quite get that."

I placed the pistol back in my pocket and struck what I took to be a menacing pose. "You talkin' to me? You talkin' to me? . . . You talkin' to me? Well, then, who the hell else are you talkin', you talkin' to me? Oh, yeah . . . Huh? Okay."

AAHH! The phone rang and I practically shot my damn foot off.

S: Uh, hello?

OS: It's me, your sister. I just called to see how things were going.

S: Ahh, okay, I guess. What's new with you?

OS: Oh, nothing. The baby's due in three weeks.

S: That's cool.

There was a silence, the infinite sad silence of long

distance. The deadly, endless silence of two siblings no longer close. I could hear my heart pounding into my ear, each breath fogged off the receiver, my right hand flexed on the wooden grips of the Colt Gold Cup. I knew there were only three options: talk about Dad, talk about the baby, talk about the weather.

OS: So, how's the weather up there?

S: Shit!

OS: What'sa matter?

S: Huh? Oh, nothing . . . uh, weather, the weather, let's see, sun comes up, sun goes down, shit like that.

OS: It's been *so* hot out here. Over a hundred.

S: How's the cow doin'?

OS: You know we didn't get a cow yet.

S: Oh, yeah.

OS: It's supposed to cool down this weekend.

S: Mmmm.

What's with the fucking weather? This weather thing was beginning to piss me off. It's some sign of the bankruptcy of society's soul. And you'd think—you'd think!—that if my family wanted to talk so much about the weather all the fucking time, then why the hell do they live in Sandy Fucking A-go, huh?! The weather never changes there. It's the same day in and day out until you fucking die a miserable San Diego Death.

OS: We're getting a new washer and dryer delivered next week. Lotta diapers.

S: I'm sure. Listen, Sis, I'm dying up here. I'm lost and I'm lonely and I don't think the planet's gonna make it. I'm afraid I might do something . . . I don't know, crazy.

OS: Doug's gonna put it in the garage.

S: Great. Has he killed anybody at work, yet? Or marked any particular supervisors for slaughter?

OS: He's been pretty busy. Oh, I saw Sianna, your old girlfriend, the other day. She's married and has a daughter now. Can you believe that?

S: Great, that makes me feel warm and fuzzy all over. Did you know that she dumped me because I never bit her nipples hard enough and didn't show the proper enthusiasm for the donning of the leather masks? At least that's what *I* think.

OS: Hunh. Well, Mom wanted me to call to see if you're okay. I don't know why she worries. I told her, "Stop worrying."

S: Mom is too nice to live with that fucking hideous criminal we call Dad.

OS: Oh, he came over yesterday to mow the lawn.

S: Daddy's *so* special. I'd like to mow him down.

OS: He gave Doug a mulcher-shredder for his birthday.

S: Awww. He gave *me* a gun, you know. It's now within my power to kill.

OS: Oh . . . so, how's work?

S: Work? Hah! Work is a lifelong soul-sapping prison. What's your view?

OS: I might go back part-time after the baby's done nursing. Mom said you're thinking of becoming a chef? I hear they make lots of money.

S: Uh, yeah, whatever. Speaking of cooking, most of the flesh seems to have cooked off the severed head I have simmering on the stove right now.

OS: We had beef Stroganoff tonight. We rented *Sleepless in Seattle*. I really like Meg Ryan.

S: Great. I sometimes watch *Natural Born Killers* over and over and over while polishing the pistol and editing my Enemies of the Realm list.

OS: Whup, that's the microwave, I guess the popcorn's ready.

S: Okay, popcorn is nice. You take care, Sis.

OS: You, too. Bye.

PO'd

A dreadful and mysterious accident seems to have taken place at the Employment Development Department. Unknowingly (unless my Fate, my Will, is at long last being tested), the EDD has sent me my latest job search referral. It's for an interview with the . . . are you ready for this shit? The United States Fucking Post Office! I can only hope that the State of California is completely, blissfully unaware of the predicament this places me in, of the deadly PO blood that boils in my veins, of the dangerous Wheel of Fortune they're spinning.

At first I couldn't help but laugh at the ridiculousness of it all. Me in my own set of Postal Blues? A pith helmet to call my very own. A few canisters of Halt (what would a good three-second blast to Carp's face affect?) at the ready. A chance to pilfer free samples.

But then . . . a morbid curiosity (an excitement?) washes over me. I see it as my grand moment of Destiny. The Fates have finally called my number. I can now realize the sick glory Dear Old Dad was too cowardly to grasp. *I* can become the latest (and possibly the greatest) Postal Worker Revenge Killer.

The EDD has no idea of the monster they'd be unleashing. The years of Hate and Blame that Dear Old Dad has instilled in me. I'll be goddamned Hitler in a postal truck: Dog tries to bite my ass? I'll shoot the cur dead on the spot. Fuck the Halt! Welfare scum complains to me—to ME?!—about his lazy fuck check being a day late? I shove him back into his house and slaughter him in his impossibly filthy kitchen. Let his seventeen cats lap at his congealing blood and gnaw at his raw flesh when he's unable to feed them.

It's a new twist. I'm not gonna kill mailmen (at least not right away), I'm gonna kill the fucking customers, man.

The job referral says something about a rural route up in Sonoma County. I'll need my own car. It sounds exciting and can only add to my later notoriety as the first Postal Serial/Revenge Killer. Can't you just see me in my beat-up Corolla, the ominously rattling muffler announcing my arrival up and down those sweet-assed roads up in Sonoma.

Dingdong! Special delivery. It's a bomb Billy and I have rigged up in The Shop. It blows away some rich assholes, but they're Volvo drivers so there's no need for sadness.

That free sample of Crest toothpaste? I wouldn't brush my teeth with it, if I were you. Shit, I could cap some cows while I'm at it.

The thing is, with my new rural route, with the invention of Steve Reeves RFD, I have a chance for the record books. Could I possibly match Edmonds? Crack the seemingly unreachable Sherrill Line?

First off, forget the senseless array of various exotic

weaponry. With my Colt (it's a fucking competition model, dude!) I don't need anything else. Just gimme five clips full of 230-grain Talons (a normally minor wound can turn fatal with the Talon's scientifically designed, jagged-mushrooming technology. The guy at the store demonstrated their wickedness by launching into some sort of Ninja claw-handed stance like he was Bob Dole imitating David Carradine. It looked scary so I bought a box).

Five clips? Thirty-five shots? Remember, I've already got a good five to ten kills on my route alone before I even turn the gun on the *mailmen*. Before I head down to the San Diego PO for a rendezvous with Dear Old Dad. I don't know Doug well enough to fantasize killing him, so I don't, but Dad's another story. I'll make him grovel and plead at his early-arrival Day of Atonement. I'll be wanting him to say how sorry he is for giving Mom shit all those years, for torturing Ole Sis, for making me what I am, but the pleas, ultimately, will fall upon deaf ears, and I'll never forget the horrified looks on the faces of all those mailmen. I cannot forget their horrified looks.

And who knows? I might even set a record (though in the minds of many San Diegans my feat would pale in comparison to James Huberty, the McDonald's Massacre Monster. The *San Diego Union*'s headline reading: "Returning Local Boy Falls Short"), but in Postal Lore my name would be whispered in hushed awe for years to come. The *second*-generation letter carrier. Son of a Mailman . . . becomes a mailman . . . and goes off. What a story! How could my normal miserable life ever hope to achieve such infamy and totality?

Let's Go Shooting

I had this dream. Shit, it was a fucking nightmare. I was in a room lit a dark neon blue. It was like some *X-Files* episode except instead of unearthly freaks, I was surrounded by a group of mailmen. Doug was there and so was Dear Old Dad. And that friend of his. The one that came over now and then and drank beer and watched football and admired Dad's gun collection. Minnefield I think was his name. He was there, too.

In this dream I'm under the hot interrogation lamps, while the mailmen stand back in the cool neon blue shadows. It seems I'm being asked to justify my actions, to explain how I could possibly turn down the RFD job. If I refuse this job, it will represent a repudiation of their entire lives. This angers the letter carriers and just as one of them reaches into a mail bag . . . I wake up, covered in a thin film of sweat. Anxious.

It's probably because today I'm meeting Dwight. Dwight Greenbaum. He's the mailman Doug has so kindly hooked me up with. Thanks, Doug. Dwight's been calling on and off for the last couple of weeks. In the messages he leaves I can always hear a dog howling in the background, or a baby wailing, maybe even a woman weeping, saying something about leaving. I cannot put Dwight off any longer and figure with my upcoming postal job interview, why not?

The range sits up near the top of the hills, above the lake, and I end up driving (The Car seemed to actually smoke slightly from under the hood when we finally arrived), but was glad I did because Dwight seemed wound a bit too tight for driving, if you ask me. Just sitting in the passenger seat on the trip out, he had the look of a man disarming a very powerful, very complicated explosive device. He had that same wiggly knee thing as Dad. The one where sitting still is just no good, so their knees work up and down like the fuckin' bobbin on a sewing machine.

We talked a bit, but because it was like some paranormal blind date, the conversation seemed stilted and forced and no one wanted to stick around very long (at least not *me* and that's who I'm talking about here). Especially when Dwight got started about how great it was what with me maybe joining "The Force" and all.

D: Rural route, huh? That's the shit. Not like the fuckin' 'burbs. That door-to-door crap. Just pull up to that bank of mailboxes. You can do it from the car. It's mostly drivin'. Waddathey payin'?

R: Huh?

D: The pay, what's the pay?

R: I think it's $9.46 and COLA. What the hell's COLA?

D: Beats me. You're an RCA, right?

R: A what?

D: Rural Carrier Associate.

R: I don't know.

D: It's part-time, right?

R: Yeah.

D: That's an RCA. They don't start you out as a fuckin' CRC!

R: CRC?

D: *Career* rural carrier.

R: Career?

D: Yeah, that's what you want.

R: It is?

D: Well . . . yeah. That's permanent. Full-time.

R: Permanent and full-time?

D: All the bennies. Retirement. Vacation. Shit, your only worry then are them damn supes.

R: Mmmm, the supes . . .

Dwight and I both nod in grave agreement concerning the dreaded supes.

We decided to limit ourselves to the pistol range that day (most mailmen, I've found, are more comfortable with a simple side arm). Dwight is packing a fairly nice Glock and I can tell he thinks it superior to my piece when I pull out the Colt. Because of this, I decide to show him no mercy and utterly humiliate him with my shooting prowess.

I've been going to the range now and then. Usually alone. I like it that way. The ammo is rather beyond my budget, but the feeling of calm and accomplishment I get from blasting fifty rounds until I entirely cut the black ring from the target cannot be measured in mere dollars and sense.

Dwight removes his jacket as we set up. His smallish hand grips the Glock way too tight. This hand is attached to a sinewy forearm that's hooked onto a muscular shoulder that's packed into a way-too-tight T-shirt that (I'm fucking not kidding. Are the gods up there having a good laugh at my expense?) has the Postal eagle emblem on it representing "Disgruntled Postal Worker's Union, Local 911." The eagle is gripping a rifle. It's kinda funny but makes me feel sad and foolish.

Dwight goes first, and while he's shooting, he tries to be funny about me living in Berkeley. All the hippies and freaks and commies. The usual shit.

D: You seem to be an okay guy for living in *Beserkeley!* I mean, when Doug mentioned you lived over there (*he shakes his head*), I figure some long-haired nut case, not mailman material.

R: I hate hippies.

D: Huh?

R: Hippies, I hate 'em.

D: Oh, yeah . . .

R: And Volvo drivers. Fuck 'em!

D: My aunt drives a Volvo.

R: Oh . . . Looks like I'm up.

I slap in the clip and release the slide lever. Empty, it makes a hollow sound, but when the Colt is packed with a full clip engaging the action, has the sound of a pair of thick handcuffs being snapped closed: serious and final.

I use a two-handed grip, firm yet relaxed. I calmly pull the pistol up to eye level and sight the bar through the notch and gently squeeze off a single round.

D: Jeez, nice shot.

It's the ten-ring, which I like, and I serenely pull the gun up again and squeeze off the rest of the clip. BOP! BOP! BOP! BOP! BOP! BOP! The sound explodes through my foam ear plugs. Three in the X, one in the nine, and the rest in the ten-ring. Dwight no longer makes fun of me living in Berkeley.

Night

Sure, I like to laugh. As much as the next guy, but sometimes things just aren't very funny. Like late at night in the dead lost silence of Cottage A. In the breathless, noiseless, amber-lit filtering dust of my shabby life. After the long day has finally spun out or the days zip by at a frantic impossible pace (impossible to keep up. I couldn't fuckin' keep up. I was falling behind). Either way, it didn't matter, you ended up the same: ultimately washed up on the sandy worn shores of late night all alone.

So quiet. I'd listen. For the sounds outside. It was very late at night before the Cedar Manor would come alive. When the coons would come scouting for food and the inevitable cat fight (hope it's not Bob gettin' his ass kicked again). When I'd hear Mrs. Park slip by under the window (creepy if you didn't think it was her). The rustling of leaves. The whoosh of a car. The lone dog that now and then moaned.

It all happened late at night. As the world crumbled

in its sleep. In the pale yellow light of my room. When a sick Fate seemed to call my name. That's when it seemed to practically glow through the wall like some sort of radioactive cache. An unfortunately newly discovered seventh sense in my brain registered its existence loud and clear. A sinister seduction.

It was at night when things would turn around in my head. When the bottom would fall out and the tears would hang in my eyes. I was Kamakazi-bound.

A hate would blossom. It would spring full-formed and foaming from the bad-brained depths of my mind. It would invade my head and then my chest. It would straighten my back and fill my lungs. I could feel it course to the tips of my fingers and then back up my arms to add more fuel to the fire.

It wasn't me when I was full to the brim with Rage. When I swelled with Tribulation terror. When I handled the gun. When I thought about Fate and the United States Post Office. When I thought of Dad.

San Diego alone had a couple of incidents, you know. There was that bloodletting up in Escondido. And, of course, there was Act Two of Black Thursday. The day two different mailmen in two different states go postal.

May 6, 1993. Black Thursday. Larry Jasion, forty-five (a twenty-three-year veteran of the force!), a mechanic at the Dearborn, Michigan, PO (the home turf of good old McIlvane, remember him?) is overcome with the virus, arms himself with a shotgun and pistol, and wastes two coworkers before, following what is becoming something of a tradition, planting a final shot in his dome. His supervisor tells reporters that Jasion, after the Edmonds, Oklahoma, slaughter in '86, had told him, "You're going to be next."

Dana Point. Meanwhile, near the Beach Boy shores

of Southern California, Mark Hilbun, thirty-eight, becomes the latest twist in Postal Killers. It seems he's *already* a psychotic killer who also happens to wear a postal uniform. His day starts out with the brutal stabbing of his mother along with her pet cocker spaniel (who I'm guessing he killed before her eyes) and then, as with Harris in New Jersey, it's off to work. He's looking for Kim Springer, a coworker he's obsessed with (he has written her a touching love note that ends with, "I love you. I'm going to kill us both and take us both to Hell.") He can't find her and only manages to kill *one* coworker, but he does have the first pet kill by a mailman so he's got to be feeling pretty good.

Then, in a second stroke of brilliance, Hilbun becomes the first Outlaw Mailman at Large! Armed and dangerous. At last, the general public is threatened by a renegade murderous fugitive letter carrier. A special detail of bodyguards is assigned the Postmaster General and an 800 number is set up for other troubled postal workers. It took like three days to find the fuckin' maniac. I kept hoping he once worked with Dear Old Dad and that Hilbun would find him, saving me from having to one day do the job.

Death and Exile

The Brady/Callahan Thang, a secret poisoned thang, was destined to one day burst into the open like a pus-filled boil. And so it did. I think the last straw was Brady getting a girlfriend. Either that or Brady getting us all eighty-six'd from The Pub. That didn't help. The Pub was more or less Cal's home away from home, not to mention the Scrabble games he *always* won.

At 12:15 the initial call comes in. I'm sitting on my porch reading the paper and drinking a cup of coffee. It's one of those breathtaking days they manufacture up in these parts of Northern California starting in September. Hanging in the air is that clear golden brilliance of fall, where, though the light is dying, almost anything seems possible.

It's Cal. He sounds kinda agitated as he offers a visit and some beer. I fall for the beer.

Cal shows up like two minutes later. Like he's made the fucking call from up on the telephone pole outside of the Manor. His six-pack is two bottles short and he appears a bit drunk, somewhat testy, and potentially fully psychotic.

After two minutes of supposed pleasantries on the porch, Callahan turns toward me slowly and has a look on his face as though he's clenching his teeth. He begins to open his mouth to speak, stops, strokes his chin pensively, readjusts his glasses, and lets out a soul-felt sigh.

My impending postal job interview has been menacing me for days now. I go in tomorrow morning, so I'm in an especially touchy mood and ask, "So what the fuck's your problem?" Callahan drains the rest of his beer in a swig and in an outrageously hateful, sarcastic voice asks, "What is it you see in Brady? Is he a *swell* guy? Is he a good man? Is he . . . *swell?*"

"Man, ya know . . ." I begin what's to be a sharp-witted aggro comeback.

"Well, I hate him," Cal interrupts. "I fucking hate him. I think he's pathetic. A punk. Patriarch of the trailer parks. A tattooed Burt Reynolds in a goatee."

"Burt Reynolds? What the hell are you talking about?"

"I just think he's disgusting. I could fucking kill him."

"Don't EVER talk to me about fucking gunplay! My old man's a fucking mailman, all right?"

"I gotta get another beer." Cal gets up and steps toward the cottage and then, in a friendly voice (like some polite lunatic, like a cross between Miss Manners and Charlie Manson, like the kind of psycho who might apologize or mop up after butchering someone), asks, "Can I get you another beer?"

"No, I'm fine." I wave him off with my bottle and it dawns on me right then that maybe, just maybe, *Sher-*

man Callahan, not me, is the lunatic in this fucking
story.

"What do you see in him?" Callahan returns with
his beer and drains almost half of it. "Huh? What is it
about ol' Brady straight from the Heart o' Te-Jas," Cal
says in an over-the-top Texas accent. "That good ol'
boy, shit kickin' spokesman for today's troubled youth?
Manna for the malignant masses . . ."

"What the fuck are you talking about, Cal? You're
so . . ."

"Oooh, anger." Cal glares at me and pushes his
tiny wire-rimmed glasses up the bridge of his nose and
then smoothes back his hair. "Reeves rushes to the de-
fense of one so precious. Look, just tell me, all right?!"

I mentally reaffirm the location of the Colt along
with a general route to it, decide odds are I can kill him
if it comes down to it, get excited at the idea of that,
and decide to press the point and see what happens.
"What the fuck do you want to know? You know what
I think the problem is . . . huh?"

"What's so great about that guy, anyway?" Cal
grimaces. "Does he amuse you? Does he bear with him
an apathetic loquaciousness of entertainment value I am
to understand?"

"I don't know what you just said, ya know?" I said.
"I don't have any idea what the fuck you're talking
about. No wonder you win at Scrabble."

"You don't know what amusing means?" The conversation is now the same affair as two starving hyenas
yankin' on either end of a half-gnawed zebra leg.

"Yeah, he's fuckin' amusing, all right? He cracks
me up."

"Ooh, Will Rogers, Jr." Cal practically jams his
glasses up his nose and through his brain. "An anec-
dotist of telling corpulence, reviling his woeful, white-

trashed allegories in a verbatim twang, supplicated by the salt of the earth gathered around his campfire in POWDUNK FUCKING TEXAS!"

"What is with you? What's your fuckin' thing!?" I look at Cal, who is nearly hyperventilating on the porch. I want so badly to say, "Yeah, but you're fully gay, right? That's what this is about, isn't it? Some homo man-love fantasy involving Brady." Instead I say, "You don't know shit."

"Oh, I know. I am more than antiquated with the incessant ramifications of his milieu. . . . I could just fucking kill him."

"Listen, if there's gonna be any fucking killing . . ."

"I want to strangle that fucking Brady."

"Cal . . ."

"Just choke him to death with my wrists on some deserted sand dune."

"With your wrists?"

"Just kill him with complete immunity . . . impunity."

"You want me to call up your dad?" I ask.

"NO!" he screams, then he readjusts his glasses, rubs his nose, takes a deep breath, and as pleasantly as though nothing at all has happened, asks, "Want to go down to The Yukon and play some shuffleboard?"

"I don't think so, buddy."

"You upset? What's the matter?"

His concern is, somehow, chilling.

"I'll buy you a beer," he offers.

"No. Cal. Thanks."

"Okay, see ya."

"What the fuck do I do now, dude?" Brady pleads with me that evening after I tell him about Callahan. We're sitting in his living room. Brady's still in his forest green Chicken Shack shirt, the paper hat with the cartoon chicken perched on his head.

"Shit, you're the bad-assed Texan. The Poodle Sawyer. Just kick his ass if he tries anything," I say.

"He fuckin' wants to kill me, dude."

"He's not gonna kill you," I reassure Brady, thinking, *I wish someone would just* try *and kill me. Boy, then.*

"That's what you fuckin' said he said."

"He's crazy!" I say this as though it is reassuring.

"Exactly, dude! He's a fuckin' secretly homosexual psycho. Wants to . . . what'd you say he wants to do?"

"Wants to strangle you with his wrists in the sand dunes."

"Oh, yeah, his wrists, dude! He's outta control. There aren't any sand dunes within a hundred miles a' here. You gotta give me that gun!"

"I ain't giving you the gun, Brady."

Brady begs for the pistol and has no idea that I'm carrying it on my person at that very moment. The holster I bought down at Seigel's works perfectly, and the pistol is completely unnoticeable under my light jacket.

"You gotta!"

"No way I'm giving you a mailman's gun. You'll just go Postal."

Brady sits for a moment, the wheels spinning in his head, his hand stroking his goatee. "Let's go find Billy."

"I ain't giving you my fucking guns, brother. No . . . mother . . . fucking . . . WAY!" Billy raged.

"Come on, Billy," Brady pleaded. "I'll pay ya."

"You just don't fucking get it, do you? Don't you see? It's right under your fucking nose, Tex, and you, too, College Boy," Billy looks at us, his eyes wild, his hair sticking out crazily from under his cap. I don't think he's slept in days. "But you freaks just don't get it. The Man . . . is after . . . ol' Billy Billingsgate. Three strikes and you're fucking out, Party Boys!" Billy's head is turning back and forth between Brady and me like he's watching a tennis match. He's nearly mesmerizing. "Billy's down in the count, that's what I'm fucking SAYING!"

Brady lets out a deep breath and shakes his head. He turns to me . . .

"No." I shake my head. "Callahan ain't gonna do nothin'."

"I was committing felonies while you punks was shittin' your pants," Billy continues his sermon. "I was slingin' crosstops when youse was watchin' *Scooby-Doo*. I was a bad-assed dude, man. Picture in the Post Office [these words capture my attention]. Hunters Point boys after my ass. Shit you cherries can't even imagine. I can't be getting caught up in your fucking penny-assed Bambi shit. Fuck!"

"Awright, just calm down, big boy," Brady tells Billy.

"Don't tell me shit," Billy says. "Those Hunters Point boys, they just don't stop, man. They're ruthless, man. Dig?" Billy salutes to his brow and snaps his hand out in a sign meaning: Brains. "And why the fuck are you wearing that stupid shit paper hat?"

"Huh?" Brady tears the Chicken Shack hat off his head and stomps up and down on it. "Come on, Billy, I'll pay ya fifty bucks."

"They don't get it." Billy looks skyward as though pleading to his methamphetamine gods and then looks about The Shop with terror in his eyes. "You boys was followed here, weren't you? You forgot to be careful. FUCK! SHIT!" Billy is now performing an enthusiastic

Speed Freak Two-Step. Back and forth. Back and forth. "DAMN! SHIT! FUCK!"

"Billy . . ." Brady begins, and I sense trouble, "shut your scrawny ass the fuck up!"

Billy looks at Brady like he remembered leaving the oven on 500 miles later. "What? . . . oh." Billy sorta laughs and maybe even smiles. "TEX!"

At the exact moment Billy yells "TEX!" he flies the six feet to Brady, wraps his hands around D's neck, and the two of them are down on The Shop floor, scrappin'.

Like an NHL referee, I let them pummel each other for a few good minutes, rather enjoying the violence. Brady gets Billy's hands quickly from offa his throat and lands a couple good Texas boy splats to Billy's sinal regions, but now Billy has Brady on the ground, bangin' his head on an oil pan. There's blood all over both of them. I think it's mostly Billy's.

Then I decide that it's my turn. "FUCKERS!" I scream and grab Billy by the shirt. Either he's much lighter than *I* even imagined or the adrenaline has rendered me near Herculean. I practically toss Billy across the floor and then, in a flash, from the hidden holster, I whip out the Colt and blast Billy's prized lava lamp to bits. The thundering sound of the weapon takes all the fight out of both boys, as I suspected it would. I'm somewhat stunned, myself, at having fired the thing and now everything seems totally crazy.

"Yeah! Dude!" Brady shouts, picking himself off the floor.

"How 'bout shutting the fuck up *just* for one minute, *just* for once, huh, D?" I ask calmly, setting the hammer carefully down to half-cocked.

"Uh . . . sure, dude."

• • •

We leave Billy cowering in the corner, sort of shoo-ing invisible insects away from himself, and Brady and I head back up the steps to the Manor.

"Dude, I can't believe you blasted that fucking lava lamp." Brady's thrilled as hell. "I fuckin' smacked that boy good a coupla times."

"I fuckin' capped Billy's lava lamp, man."

"I know, that's what I'm sayin'. That was hella cool, dude."

"When he comes to, it's gonna be like fuckin' OK Corral here between me and Billy."

"Billy ain't gonna do shit," Brady reassures me. "You're Alpha Dog now, dude."

Then I hear sirens. Sirens coming close and then closer still and then I hear them stop right outside, and I imagine Billy or Carp's called the cops. I see the flashing red lights in the twilight sky: red and it's trouble. I'm sure I've been immediately caught and I'm afraid of what may happen next.

But it's not cops, it's an ambulance and two guys in white come running up with a gurney and head to Mrs. Park's cottage. In a second they have her on that gurney, still as can be. Francisco, this little Colombian guy who was her man, is in tears, shaking his head as he asks me in broken English if I can take him to the hospital.

Francisco looks so small in the harsh light of the hospital as he stands there, a stunned, pink-eyed, frozen eternity. It was a stroke. The doctor says it's in a bad spot. That she's not gonna make it to morning. I feel sick to my stomach as I look one last time at Mrs. Park as she lies on the bed, tubes coming out of her nose and mouth, but a peaceful look on her face. So very relaxed and calm. It's the first time I've ever seen her hair down; she always kept it up in a bun. It's very long and jet black with strands of silver.

Back at my place there are some messages on the answering machine.

BEEP! It's Billy. "Watch your back, fucker."

BEEP! It's Cal. "I'm just callin' to say I'm t-taking the night train to N-new Mexico. I g-got some friends there. Th-they got a restaurant. I'll send you a p-postcard."

BEEP! "Hi, it's Mom. I just called to see how you were doing. Hope everything's nice. Call me . . . bye."

BEEP! "Hey, Steve, this is Dwight. Greenbaum. Good luck on your interview tomorrow. I know a couple of the boys up there. Good guys [a howling dog and colicky baby can be heard in the background]. They'll make sure, would you shut him the fuck up?! Can't you see I'm on the phone? Sorry, kids, heh-heh. Look, gimme me a call and just remember, that a mailman, shut that kid up, damn! And put the, hey! the dog, Sam! Oh shit. Look, I gotta go. Gimme a call."

It was all coming to a head. My life at last had some sense of immediacy, and I didn't like it. Remember back at Drunk Before Noon? How that seemed like way too much shit happening all at once? Well, this . . . this is way worse. Way the fuck worse. It's like a fucking joke. First Cal. And this mailman thing tomorrow. Brady and Billy brawlin'. Shootin' a fuckin' gun? Mrs. Park.

Oh, god. Mrs. Park. Each time I thought her name I saw her there in that hospital room and then alive walking about the neighborhood with her sweater wrapped about her. I'd remember her with a handful of plums and near vomit up a tear in one heave, try to swallow it back (it'd make my eyes well) and then I'd think of me and Love so long gone and Mrs. Park dead and gone and then I wept, broke down and rock bottomed.

Mrs. Park was gone. Love was lost. The gods were dead. The heroes committed suicide. I couldn't believe it as I sat in my cottage. So close to hers, but no more. The thought of the famous plums was killing me. The doorstep dim sum, the crazy water conspiracy. Why hadn't I just listened to her? Why did I feel I didn't have the time or that it was so bothersome? I wished so bad right then for her to be back to tell me once more about it. How glad I would be to listen now. Now that it was too late.

I called Mom for reasons I could hardly admit. I wanted to say how lost and lonely and sad I was. I wanted her to make it better like she used to when I was little, but it just didn't happen. Once on the phone I turned tongue-tied, and she was her usual emotionally distant self.

M: Oh, I made those cookies you like.

S: Huh?

M: You know. Those chocolate ones.

S: With the mint filling?

M: Yes, you still like those, don't you?

S: Yeah.

M: And the coconut ones, too. Dad's gonna mail them tomorrow.

I realized then that Mom was speaking to me through those cookies. That the cookies were how she showed she still loved her boy. The chocolate mint ones meant she still thought about me and the sugar ones with the fake colored icing meant Family because they were *her* mother's recipes. Love and nurture passed down from the rich dairy fields of Wisconsin.

As I thought these thoughts, as the receiver crackled in the long-distance silence, I could feel Mom there, feel her like I hadn't in years, and I wanted so badly to tell her I loved her. That I missed her . . . but I just couldn't, and I swallowed back emotions that near choked me.

M: Well, I guess that's all down here. It was nice of you to call.

S: Yeah.

Yeah, was all I said, but in my mind it meant all those other things and more. But it was just a "yeah." A bullshit filler.

M: I guess I better let you go.

S: Okay, Mom. Uh . . . Bye.

I hung up the phone and the words were stuck in my craw. Like a fish bone that would slowly kill me. I love you. What the fuck is wrong with me?

I opened my bedroom window to try and get some air, I was so empty and hurting. It seemed so dark that night, and I waited for Cedar Manor to come alive, for the coons to come out, for Bob to show up at my window, for the jasmine-scented cool night air to drift into my window. I waited for Mrs. Park to walk by on one of her midnight missions.

Sleep was impossible as I tossed and turned and my mind ached and raged and soon everything became simply anger. Everything went black. I decided to take a walk.

I headed up the hill. To the Brady Bunched streets up Northside. Just above the Seedy Manor. I walked the sweet streets in the pitch black. I looked in the windows, in the many late-night windows that still glowed so warm homey yellow. I had the gun. I'm not sure why.

I don't know why, but I was simply compelled, as I left my cottage, to bring along the Colt. It was as though the thing had some sort of control over me as I slipped it into the deep hip pocket of my purple overcoat. I had six in the clip and one in the chamber.

I wandered these dark streets an impoverished soul, fully clothed and housed, yet impoverished nonetheless. I looked into those lit-up windows, with the nice wood, all those Northside houses with the nice wood paneling and the antique furniture. And all the books. Always the wall of books.

The fuckers. They've got it all. They got the good jobs, the big house, the new car, traveling 'round the world like it ain't shit. The things I was supposed to want. The things I didn't have.

I hated them. I hated them all and some of them aren't even assholes. They're professors or writers and because I have no reason to hate them, I hate them even more because of my own self-hate for not having such things. For being a failure. I was tired of being a failure. I was tired of being on the outside looking in. I was tired of waiting.

But my poverty lay not only in my borderline economic disaster waiting to happen, but in a spiritual wastedness that cut to my very soul. It sucked the very breath out of me that night. I was fucking suffocating.

I felt somehow empty inside my own body. As

though it were hollow and fake yet at the same time I was hyper-aware of everything: my hand gripping the pistol, the sweat beading on my brow, the racing anxiety deep within my breast, the smell of the honeysuckle and a skunk not long gone.

As I walked aimlessly, my mind spun and seethed. I had the gun out now. It seemed natural as I looked into the windows from the sidewalks I prowled, fever-brained and lost. You'd think a pane of glass might deflect a bullet, but it doesn't. It'll go right through. Right through to that man crossing his living room to-night.

The streets were empty and lifeless, but whole worlds were happening behind the lit windows that late night. Lives unreal and despised. Yet coveted.

I passed a window and Shorter! No, it was a man who looked just like him. I pulled the pistol slowly up to eye level. Fuck this guy. In the dark, he was lit up like a video game. My head was swimming with violence. I could barely swallow, my tongue was so thick and dry. I quietly cocked the pistol. I pictured the fat cartridges. The impressive heft of a single one in the palm of your hand. Two hundred and thirty grains. At twenty-five feet I can't possibly miss.

My mind sizzles, my heart pounds, my hand trembles.

This is the moment I've supposedly been waiting for. My face flushes. I feel red hot prickly. The skin on the back of my neck is literally cooking. Here's my chance. My head begins to eye roll spin to near collapse.

Pap. Pap. I imagine capping him dead. I put the pistol back into my purple overcoat, my hand clenched upon the grip. I'm almost ready.

I walk on, imagining better game up ahead. It's all so random, I can't help but smile. I might even get away with it. The gun's virtually untraceable. If I make it back home . . . I pick up the pace as I see the next lit window, a few houses down. Who will it be?

But in the next house there was a girl. Just a girl and she was sitting in the kitchen and so late, too. And then a boy came in, her brother probably. Two kids. They were just sitting in the kitchen smiling. Innocent. I remembered how Ole Sis and I would play late at night when Mom and Dad went out. The sweet fun we had. The good sister she was.

I felt loathsome and shameful. A new seed erupted momentarily in my brain. A seed of Hope long lost. A picture of Mom in my head.

My mind was racing, making no sense. What is it I want? The problem is, I just don't know. I no longer understood how Ole Sis could be pleased as punch to simply create *her* version of suburban life. The satisfaction she got from her hardworking husband, the joy at owning her own house, the rapture when she delivers her beautiful baby boy. I didn't begrudge her this, I just didn't get it. The pretty picture of me in that situation left me dazed and gasping for air.

Yet I could no longer pretend the problem was that my family didn't understand me, that society didn't appreciate me. The problem ran much deeper than that. *I* didn't understand me. *I* didn't appreciate me. I needed some sort of guidance. I needed the gods to intervene and issue me tasks that I couldn't question, tasks in whose completion I would ultimately realize myself. I *needed* voices in my head directing me onward. As it stood, life was too bewildering a prospect. It could be anything. Or nothing. Anything. Nothing.

I was now scraping the bottom for certain. I'd been cut free from all moorings. My hours and days now played out endlessly, making no sense whatsoever. I have nothing to believe in. I have no faith. I've been cut off from the gods, estranged from my family, alienated from society, yanked from my primeval forests and dropped down in the middle of a twenty-first-Century Concrete Nightmare Playground of creature comforts and unspeakable horror that leaves me, finally, stunned and disamused.

Maybe I'm just suicidal. Maybe I'm fucked up in a way that, since I'm so fucked up, I've figured wrong all along. I'm in serious need of some answers. Something to guide me out of this wilderness. I need burning bushes and Rosetta stones immediately!

I ached for some sort of meaning (if only I were a Calvinist. If only I could clutch to my chest a predestination that shone golden and clear). Something that would resonate deep within my breast. Something to satisfy a primal hunger whose stomach growled uneasily in the center of my brain. Something *other* than death and destruction.

As I walked farther and farther on, as I kept flexing my hand on the Colt stashed in my pocket, I realized my life had reached a crisis point. It couldn't keep going on like this. Something had to give. I felt like a murderous Conquistador on Cortez's Conquest of Mexico. There was no turning back. The ships lay in smoldering ruin and the march to Tenochtitlán was the only choice. Instead of Gold, I sought . . . Love. It was a kiss I was dying for. A pair of arms around me, a smile to lose myself in. A warm kiss was all that could save me. Nothing else made sense in this senseless, horrific world we'd created, but Love still reigned supreme. Let Love reign over me. Someone help me!

When I saw the pay phone, I knew what I needed to do. I picked up the receiver. My arm could barely manage the weight. With great effort, I lifted it to my ear as I fumbled through my pockets for change.

FUCK! No fucking change! Can't I ever have what I fucking want when I fucking need it? Just once? I'm now near insane and for the first moment ever, I wonder if I shouldn't just kill myself.

And then I remember and the thought almost makes me laugh. It was so absurd. My entire life had become so absurd. Who else to call at this final hour, at the Dawn of the Third Millennium, at the Gates of Doom? I fish the package out of my pocket and call: 1-800-622-4726.

It rings maybe three times and then picks up. There's a flash of silence and then . . . music and that name.

Naa-bi-scoo. Pling.

It's the Nabisco Hot Line. The Twenty-Four-Hour Oreo Crisis Management Task Force. As it rang again, how I hoped for deliverance from all this hell in the hands of the friendliest white-haired lady I could imagine in that blackest-before-the-dawn moment. She'd have the dearest smile, with cat-eyed glasses and a sweater draped over her frail shoulders. It's Team Norman Rockwell. The kind of folks that still care.

N: Nabisco. How are you today?

R: Uh, not so good, I guess.

N: Have you had a problem with one of our products?

She sounds so very concerned that I almost weep.

R: No, I love Oreos. They're America's greatest cookie.

227

N: Oh, good. That's nice of you to say.

R: Yeah, I love 'em.

N: Would you like to hear about how Oreos came about?

R: Sure. I think I'd like that.

N: Well, they were introduced in 1912, and the name comes from either the French "ore" for gold, or the Greek word for mountain, "oreo."

R: It means mountain?

N: Why, yes, and the original cookie was hill-shaped.

R: Hell-shaped?!

N: No, *hill* shaped. Like a triangle.

This tidbit of information makes me feel better, and I ask why they changed to round.

N: I don't know, but I kind of like them round.

R: Yeah, me, too.

N: Can I send you a packet all about Oreos and some free coupons?

R: Free coupons?

N: Sure.

She sounded so nice. I remembered Mom and Gramma. Oreo coupons on the way. I gave the lady my address as though confessing my sins to the Father. I was so very tired as I hung up the phone. It was then I noticed I was one block from the lumberyard and the first light of dawn ran along the Grizzly Peak horizon.

My anger was fading. I was so very tired. I wasn't

going to that Post Office interview. I didn't care if I lost my unemployment benefits. I just *wasn't* mailman material after all.

I stood there, in front of the lumberyard, alone in the first light of dawn, just me and the initial birds that late-summer morning. Sweaty, tired, lost, and alone. No change in my pocket, only a few dollars. I was an immigrant just landed upon a new day's shore. Broke with only Hope. I could still have Hope if I wanted. No one could ever take that away from me.

A beat-up old pick-up makes a mad U-turn half a block up. The tires squeal as the truck makes a quick U and wheels toward me. As the truck rapidly closes the distance between us, my no-sleep, addled brain imagines this U-turn involves me directly, that it is *me* this truck on this particular moment has targeted. I imagine it's the cops, undercover detectives, intelligence agents sent by the Postmaster General. Though I've yet to do anything, I feel arrest is now imminent, and I'm almost glad. I just want to go to sleep.

The truck has now come to a stop before me. The man inside the truck seems to be leaning toward me. As though underwater. The window rolls down like molasses. My hand clenches the pistol as one last image of murder crosses my mind. I'm practically shaking and tears fill my eyes as I decide to save two lives. I let the pistol go. It drops into the depths of my pocket, and I feel a wave of shame as I realize I *can't* do it. I don't want to. I picture Dear Old Dad; he's disappointed again.

Dear Old Dad. There he was again. It was as though he were the technician who wired me, the Frankenstein who created me. It was as though, that night, I had become him. I saw my despair in his bitterness. I doubted myself for his disappointments. I was lost in the face of his anger. I heard his voice in my own. He has tricked me to fail.

The window completes its interminable journey downward, a smile appears on the man's face, and I imagine that I've just saved his life. He leans toward me and cackles like a madman, "Ahh-hah-hah-hah-hah, a white boy. Far out. Want some work? Eighty dollars a day."

A strong gust of wind blows up the street from the bay as I look into this man's eyes. They're baby blue and clear. The breeze has a slight salt smell of the ocean, and it's cool, fresh, and green. It slips by quickly under my nose, through my hair, cooling the soaked armpits of my midnight madness. I look to the east. The sky is crystal clear. No fog. Just a few wispy clouds, way up high. The sun seems to be shining this morning. It looks like it's going to be one of those days. One of those beautiful days.

"Uh . . . sure," I say and jump in. I'm drenched in sweat. My face is still afire. I nervously feel the weight of the Colt in the coat. I'm afraid I might just burst into tears.

The man doesn't seem to notice a thing. Nothing seems at all strange to him. He simply smiles a Mad Hatter's smile, tears the top off a bag of chocolate M&Ms, pours about half into his mouth, and guns the truck up into the Oakland hills.

"Now, my mother, dear old Mom, named me Tim. Timmy. Little Timmy Thomas from Tiburon." He grinned at me madly, shaking his head back and forth in tiny little shakes. "I was Timmy all my school years and then, when I went to Cal—studied in philosophy you understand—well, one day I realized I wasn't Tim.

That dear old Mom didn't know what she was doing. It was revealed to me—I was taking a lot of acid in those days—ahh-hah-hah-hah-hah!—that I was Morgan."

I wasn't exactly sure what he was saying. I was convinced that by now he would have looked at me and known something wasn't right. He'd begin to ask me questions, and then I'd break down and confess it all (even though there was still nothing to confess, I was still greatly troubled). I'd have the gun on me and be arrested and now all I wanted more than anything was to just get rid of the fucking gun and stop with all this craziness once and for all. Now I wanted to survive. I wanted to win. I wanted something good to happen. I wanted to ignore the poison Dad had planted in my brain. If I could just get some sleep.

"I went through a few, you know. Morgans." He turned to me happily chomping on his morning's M&Ms. "Morgan, Morgan 4, Morgan 11 . . . Morgan 17! So now, when I talk to clients or do my paperwork or my taxes, I'm still Tim, but really, with someone like you, I'm Morgan 17." He smiled at me as though he had just explained some heretofore unknown workings of the cosmos. Then he leaned toward me and lowered his voice so that I could hardly hear him, especially in my bad ear. "And Morgan can be a very naughty boy. Ahh-hah-hah-hah-hah!"

His mad laugh made me feel somehow better. There was something soothing about collapsing into the soft seat of his pick-up. I didn't want to kill anyone. I didn't even want to *work* at the post office. As I felt the weight of the gun hanging in my coat pocket, I realized that the only person I might have shot that night would have been myself. Or Dear Old Dad.

• • •

"You know, you're the first person I've hired in years that wasn't either an illegal or a lesbian." Then he cackled that Morgan 17 cackle. "Ahh-hah-hah-hah-hah. Years!"

I swallowed back once more, my eyes filled with fat tears, and I remembered: Clouds in the Heavens. The superior man stands up to his Fate. That's what it said. It was time to stand up to my Fate.

"Wanna donut?" Morgan asked and tilted a white paper bag toward me.

I was hit with the smell of them. Sweet and sugary. Doughy and fresh. I saw a devil's food chocolate cake with the fudge icing. Those used to be my favorites when I stayed at Gramma's house after school. She always had a couple ready when I arrived. It was like a secret of sorts from Dear Old Dad. The idea of eating a donut in the middle of the day pissed him off to no end. I reached in for that donut.

"Thanks," I said and took the biggest fucking bite I could without actually cramming. I chomped upon it with the greatest delight, my soul now light, the night having passed. "You like Oreos?"

"Ah! One of the finest cookies ever created." He shook his head in respect. "You got any?"

We both laughed, and I felt good again. Like the time I had that fever. When it finally passed, how alive simply being weak in bed felt. I felt *that* alive right then, the window rolled down a crack, the eucalyptus-scented morning's shadowed breeze filling my lungs with a rejuvenating freshness. I asked, "What kind of work we doin'?"

"Oh, demolishing a bathroom." Morgan seemed to accelerate the truck at this thought. "Wait'll you see this house. Magnificent. Just don't work too hard. Aah-ha-ha-ha-ha!"

232

Morgan 17

After that first day of work, work that seemed to bring me back to a semblance of reality, Morgan invited me into his house to pay me. He offered me a can of soda, a hit off one of his endless post-work Rasta spliffs, and some candy from his collection he had strewn across his cluttered coffee table.

Apparently Morgan 17 regularly went to CostCo and bought every twenty-four-count box of candy bar ever concocted by the Mars Corporation.

Being a philosopher of some seriousness, Morgan explained his theory concerning the Mars Corporation and Proctor & Gamble (the well-known, according to Morgan, Satanic personal hygiene products company). He considered their association as being rather mysterious and probably malevolent. And his proof?

"They both use celestial symbols in their logos. Ah-hah-hah-hah-hah! Like they're fooling anybody." Morgan shot me his madman smile. "One makes candy and the other makes toothpaste? Come on!" And then he proceeded to empty another half bag of M&Ms into his mouth. "I *still* can't believe they put blue ones in. Blue M&Ms! Who ever heard of such a thing? Ah-hah-hah-hah-hah!"

And so Morgan 17 became my newfound boss. My stack of twenty-dollar bills on Friday employer. Oh sure, he might be stark raving mad. Gramma was an anti-Semite. Callahan was secretly bisexual, possibly secretly homosexual. Brady and Billy were racist homophobes. Whatever! At last, at last! I had a boss who didn't feed off castigating workers, who didn't revel in yelling at the underlings. It was fat paydays and happy workdays.

It was still work, to be sure, but it gave form to my day. It gave me a sense of purpose. The hauling of hundreds of pounds of tools up the seventy-seven steps to Mrs. Montgomery's upstairs bathroom tired my muscles and calmed my mind. The twenty-two pieces of Sheetrock maneuvered up the stairs, careful not to ding the walls or antique furniture at the Raftons', who had the biggest damn house I've ever seen in my life (oh, what a grand life the Raftons must have! Would that I were that rich, I marveled) gave me at least a tiny sense of accomplishment. The 376 weathered red bricks unloaded and stacked to make Mrs. Lundquist's Tuscan-style kitchen with wood-burning pizza oven, finished in a half day, had Morgan paying me a bonus.

I'd work the strangest hours with Morgan. It'd be three days one week, then nothing for a full week until an intense four-day session where we'd work ten to twelve hours a day, and I'd go home with five hundred dollars. Cash! A couple of days like that, and I walked the streets of Berkeley well-hung, with a smile on my face, my muscles satisfyingly sore, my head up, a wad in my pocket, and money, too.

The world had changed. A high-rollermanship filled my heart like a flower-strewn spring meadow. At last I had money! I was suddenly catapulted into an economic level that seemed inconceivable a mere two weeks before. I had Anchor in the fridge! I ate meals that didn't involve meat between a bun or glop wrapped in a big flour tortilla. My black moods faded with sore muscles and money in my pocket. I again dreamt of Hope.

And it was all simply Chance. A new Fate. A different Destiny. Dumb Luck. Morgan 17. My wrecky angel in the battered Toyota pick-up delivering me from a Postal Hell. A chocolate–M&Ms–popping Gabriel. For it was he, it was Morgan 17, who handed me the brown-eyed girl. And this girl suddenly? Well, isn't that how it always is?

Pie

Brady and I were sitting at a booth in Nicely's in the beat strip of town on the far side of the Sierra known as Lee Vining. We each had a cup of steaming coffee before us and were waiting for a slice of pie. We'd already polished off our big Hungry Man breakfasts we required after our one night up in Yosemite: eggs over easy, strips of crunchy, crumbly bacon, potatoes, and a stack of white bread toast. Nicely's at that moment was the epitome of civilization to us: breakfast, coffee, a jukebox, and pie on the way.

I couldn't wait for my slice. I'd heard they had a fine pie over at Nicely's, fresh made. After our great camping adventure and a few hours on the road like we'd had, pie takes on all sorts of significance that it never has when you're just standing still. During our long-awaited trip to Yosemite (at long last leaving the Bay Area), throughout our race up the mountains from the valley (the dusty San Joaquin towns giving way to the graceful pine forests), in the crisp fall air and the brilliant fading light of glorious new October, my un-requited Pie Lust had grown to immense proportions—as big as the horizon before us. The farther out we got, with each mile we covered, so grew the implications, the gravity, the importance of Pie.

"I remember one time Rachel and I had this pie," I said, taking another sip of coffee. "It was in the south."

"They make the best pie down there," Brady agreed.

"It was in southern Arkansas or northern Louisiana and the woman had *just* made it. It was fresh baked, not ten minutes out of the oven."

"What kind?"

"Pecan. A dollar twenty-five a slice, and the lady'd just made it. Man, that was pie."

"Why'd you order peach then?"

"Well, you can't just order pecan from anybody," I said. "Pecan in the wrong hands?" I shook my head.

"Yeah, I guess that's true, dude. My mom could make a good pecan pie."

"Really?"

"Shit yeah."

"Oh, man, I wish I could try it sometime."

"Sure. You gotta go to Texas first, dude."

The waitress returned with our slices of pie, and Brady and I dug in. After we finished, Brady pushed the plate away and leaned back in his seat with a look of grand satisfaction on his face. "Pie on a beautiful day like this. After last night, dude? Kinda makes a dude happy to be alive."

I was.

The night before, we'd spent up in the park. Up Tuolumne way. Out by Porcupine Flat. We'd hiked in a ways, just out of sight of the road. It was no backpacking adventure. We had far too much beer for that. We'd filled our packs with bits of food and water, our sleeping bags and pads, some coffee and a small, thin pot for making it, some smokes, and pen and paper just in case, and the rest of our packs were devoted to twenty-eight bottles of beer along with the special bag of vintage magic mushrooms Morgan 17 gave me.

As the sun faded below the tree line, Brady and I sat in a quiet forest glen just above the scattered granite erratics. We'd eaten the Morgan stash, nearly gagging on it, and sat sipping our beers anxiously awaiting the Word of God.

After a while, Brady announced, "I ain't feelin' nothin.' I don't think Morgan's stash is packin' anything, dude."

"I don't know," I said, "I'm feeling a little funny in the back of my throat."

"Sure is beautiful up here," Brady said.

"Yeah. I told you. California is amazing."

"That it is." Brady lit a cigarette.

Cloud's Rest and Quartzite Peak had blushed a pale and serene pink as the sky deepened. Half Dome, off down the valley, hung in the shade, holding its gray hues of solid granite.

I was soon hypnotized by Cloud's Rest. By its sheer bulk, by all the sunlight it reflected in the sun's last glory before nightfall. It looked as though it had been formed out of beaten bronze. Its steep, monumental face chipped and sculpted into Thor's own shield.

It was the work of gods, I thought, as my entire being slipped quietly into the sounds of the forest. The wind. The rustling leaves. No birds. The smell of the pines. The vacuum presence of irresistible Nature in all its might.

As I lay on the ground, melting away, my being

soaking into the earth, all that remained was the still-warm air languidly rushing by. The color show of the setting sun. The mountain's majesty. God shed his grace.

Brady and I looked at one another. Without saying a word, we nodded and knew. We were gone to the magic of Morgan's Magic Stash, and now we were laughing. Laughing and rolling on the granite floor. Laughing and laughing so hard. Some joke about Carp and the hot tub.

I lay on my back, my temples wet from the tears of laughter, a deep breath and all became still. I was again absorbed by the place. Cloud's Rest was now gray, returned to the earth and its shadows. I lay on the granite floor, more comfortable than you would imagine, and melted into the landscape. Drawing power from the earth. From the rare air. From the rocks. From the living smells of the pines.

Everything fit just then. All made sense again. Out here, on the perimeter, there were no questions. Everything had its place. All was proper. Each and every twig and pebble a microcosm of the whole, a reflection of the possibilities of perfection.

As I thought all this (Brady silently lying not ten feet away but a universe removed), I noticed a small, pink stone. It stood out amid all the gray, and I picked it up and held it in my palm as though it were Communion. I took a drink from my water bottle and there it all was. In that moment. In my hand. In the form of that pink pebble. The World. The Earth. Heaven above, and then I noticed all the stars now out, flashing in the dark blue sky. It was a dark blue that glowed and hugged you like a favorite warm blanket on a cold winter night, a few wispy clouds drifting by, far above. I again remembered Clouds in the Heaven. With sincerity comes Light and Success. I remembered it as a truth long forgotten. A road back home after having been so long lost. And there before me lie the possibilities of perfection. A sweet life to be had.

It seemed like we were lying there for hours, lifetimes, like we'd journeyed to the Ends of Time and returned to tell the tale and we snapped out of our dreamy calm, comfortable, smiling-faced reverie and got up as though our bodies were returned to us at last or that, now, we finally again had use for them.

"Woooh man," Brady said, shaking his head. "That was something."

"Yeah, Jesus," I said.

"I'm gonna build me a fire," Brady said, rubbing his hands together eagerly, looking like he'd just woken from a long nap.

As he built the fire (and Brady could build a fire quicker and easier than anyone I'd ever watched, a few twigs, some bigger sticks, a scrap of paper, and a single match, and soon he had a couple of small logs crackling) true night fell and the stars were spectacular and the yellow warm glow of the fire was primal and satisfying.

"Back there I kept thinkin'," Brady said, "if there really was a god, why would he allow us to visualize things we cain't have?"

"You mean grant your every desire?"

"No! I ain't sayin' . . . well, yeah. Exactly, dude. Is that so wrong?"

"You'd just want someting else," I said.

"Yeah . . . and then you'd get it."

"I don't know." For some reason all I could think of right then was *Bonanza*. Lorne Greene riding up on that horse. "You know the Cartwrights lived around here."

"Huh?"

"Cartwrights. *Bonanza*."

"No way, dude. They're from Texas. Ain't no cowboys up here."

"No, man. Where the fuck do you think the Ponderosa was, anyway?"

"Yeah?"

"Yeah. Lake Tahoe. Remember the map they lit up starting every show?"

"Hmmph." Brady nodded and nudged a stick around in the fire, his face lit red and orange. "I never watched it much."

"Me, neither. They were so straight."

"Yeah, dude. Fuckin' candy-assed Lake Tahoe cowboys."

"Yeah," I agreed. "I guess they weren't that tough."

"No way. They were pussies, dude. Clint Eastwood could kill all of 'em, no problem. Little Joe? Come on!"

"Frat boy cowboys," I said.

"Fuckin' Lake Tahoe, frat boy, candy-assed cowboys, dude."

The night passed dreamily, lovely, calm, and comfortably. A million sights, a million sensations. Love was again my god. The crackling, dying campfire my ally. Mrs. Park I did honor with a small tear. I felt the weight of past mistakes drift away into the limitless crisp October night sky above Porcupine Flat. My body and mind were calm, weightless, serene. Life was sweet. Love would come. Clouds in the Heavens.

In the morning, we boiled up our coffee, we broke our camp, we headed back to The Car, which started right up and headed down the east side of the Sierra. Through the Tioga Pass and down the Tioga Grade to

Lee Vining. I fished the pink rock out of my pocket as we dropped down into the barren rain shadow in the east. The little pebble didn't look nearly so miraculous in the light of Next Day. Its pinks not so precious, but the truths it revealed in the glorious night seemed untarnished and reassuring, and I thought about what kind of pie I might have.

love

The girl! It happened so fast as to catch me by surprise, yet ready as though I'd waited all my life. The Brown-Eyed Girl. Delivered to me by Morgan 17 one day, an unforeseen gift. Salvation walked into the room unknowing in the form of a perfect, just-right-for-me, ripe-shouldered girl. Her eyes soft and moist. Nervous and smiling. Friendly and quiet.

It was a job in Orinda. Morgan was hired by a certain Mr. Williams to knock out a perfectly fine kitchen and replace it with an even *more* perfect, *more* fine one. Wolff stove, handmade, rain forest–friendly wooden cabinets, Italian marble tiles, even some hand-painted ones.

"These cost fifty dollars each," Morgan told me in a very low voice as I admired the beautiful tiles painted with images of fish and kelp. "Fifty dollars! Ah-hah-hah-hah-hah."

The crew was assembled, and because the family would be vacationing for the next two weeks on some extra-special island off the coast of Greece, Morgan came up with the brilliant idea that we would work and live in the house for the next four to five days. Each night after a good day's work, whip up dinner, drink beers, smoke bud (Morgan 17 smoked bud like no other man. He lit up like a fuckin' Rasta, like he'd been born and bred in Jamaica, like he was training for a place on the team for the Marijuana Games), watch videos on the massive 900-inch TV, and sleep on the entertainment room floor in our sleeping bags.

The crew included Morgan, myself, a lesbian couple, Maxie Campos from Guadalajara (Happy Maxie we called him, Happy Maxie with the gold tooth display) and, of course, the Brown-Eyed Girl.

Stacy. Sweet Stacy. What an exciting, sexy name it seemed to me. Magical. Lyrical. It was the best name ever, and why had I never heard it before?

Stacy was born in Hollywood of all places and she had the strong- and long-limbed, healthy tanned look of the girls who grow up in the southern part of the state, from around Santa Barbara on down (there *is* a line, you know). A California Girl she was, sprung from the same sidewalks and trimmed lawns that I had known. The kind of girl engineered on the white sand beaches of Huntington, Zuma, Doheny, and Del Mar. The kind of girl dreams are made of. My first sight of her near took my breath away and I *knew*, or at least *hoped*.

And what did we say to each other that nervous, mind-spinning first day of work together? The words that aroused the possibility of all that I hoped and imagined? I can't say for sure, it was just the usual bio factoids of past, the dreamed-for faith in futures brighter. The exchange of various taste ratings and laundry listings of things loved and loathed: which bands were good, which politicians sucked, our respective stances on Pete Wilson, cigarettes, red meat, and hippies.

And after that first day of work, after working by her side, after realizing that it was Morgan 17 who wanted her and had hired her out of a hope-she's-not a-lesbian, hope-she'll-fuck-me dream, after sitting out on the Williamses' beautiful back porch, sipping beers in the stunning October dusk, after those little signs and imagined messages (Can it be true? Does she like me, or am I just dreaming?) we laid down our sleeping bags not three feet from each other, watched a movie (I swear to you I cannot remember what it was, my mind was lost on her), and ended the night face-to-face, talking quietly. It was the most comfortable thing I'd ever imagined. She had the dreamiest voice, rich and luxuriant. And the fullest lips. They seemed like Home.

"I gotta get some sleep. Good night," she said at last with a sweet smile and turned her soft shoulders, and I watched her as she gently filled and subsided with each soft breath. I was in Love. I was lost. I was excited. I was terrified.

My mind spun and soared. It filled with Joy and then with Fear. It was all possible . . . and then not! Yet the spell was impossible to resist. It came over me in a sleepy warmth, my mind fuzzy and comfy, my stomach going down that first giant descent on the roller coaster up at Six Flags.

It was all I could do but to think of her all night long. Near impossible to sleep, my bag seemed to cook my very flesh. Sweat beaded upon my brow. I thought I might be getting sick. Fear and longing too much to even consider transformed my sleeping bag into a fevered raft tossed helplessly about.

Love. Lust. Infatuation. She wants me. She loves

me! She doesn't. She loathes me. Who would want me? Ahh, what's the use?

But can't it be? Can't sweet, intoxicating love be within my reach at last in the form of lovely Stacy? Can't something work out, just for once? We got along so well today. I'm sure it's *me* she's singled out.

But I don't know. I know Morgan hired her with designs of his own, but he doesn't know his role. This is Fate: meeting Morgan, this job, him hiring Stacy. It was all meant for this. For me. For us. To be together, Stacy and I. Isn't it?

I asked my brain all these questions, but it was no use. I had no answers and so the fevered raft of my sleeping bag tossed and turned as I lay motionless (my brain flying about) until, finally, sometime before dawn, I drifted off to sleep.

The next morning, Maxie whipped up some papas y huevos and it was off to work. Stacy immediately seemed extra quiet and distant, and Morgan put me on some work detail far from the action. I watched him joke and cajole her. God, how I hated him and then the two of them.

My mind was Postal and poisoned as I hung up drywall and nail-gunned the tiny strips of window molding. I went about my work that day bitter and sour, falling victim to the evil seed of Dear Old Dad. Knowing all was no use. Knowing all was for naught. Knowing nothing ever worked out right. It was all I could do to not simply walk off the job.

But it was all I could do but to think of her all day long till it made me sick in the pit of my stomach and broke at the core of my breast fast upon the heels of imagined sweet love blossoming new in my soft and vulnerable heart. I suffered an ache and lostness for my unrivaled imaginings of love true and sudden captured in the sparkling dark eyes and sweet red smile of this girl.

I remembered Yosemite. The pink stone. My lesson was sincerity. And, like a miracle, it was all good again. Stacy helped me make spaghetti for the second night's meal, and she quietly told me she thought Morgan was completely insane. And we agreed, with a quiet laugh, that he was mad, but nice, that he was good, but odd, and now we were pals again and by the third evening, it was as though we had been childhood friends. Like we'd known each other a lifetime. We seemed drawn to each other, tentative and desiring, a nervous longing.

And finally a kiss or I think we would have both exploded. It happened that third evening out on the sagging brick wall in the Williamses' backyard. The clear-as-a-bell October evening's sky sparkled with the first stars and Venus and a sliver of moon up by Grizzly Peak. We sat by each other, first talking and then quiet. I was dying for her in the dark blue light of dusk. I couldn't resist.

A sweet kiss. Yes, it can be true, a kiss can save you. A soft, lingering kiss (and I swear she tasted of peaches) for the ages, my eyes closed and hers, too. Her full lips carried me away that evening to the place I needed to go. It was Heaven. Love can take you there.

Well, the next day, Morgan seemed to know what was up, and he looked none too happy, and at lunch break he said that we had to go. He seemed rather upset and a little depressed. He handed us our pay and a few extra twenties, 'cause that's the kind of guy he was, and he said:

"I'm sorry, but I just can't do this. I'm reasonable and I'm rational, but please, please, I don't want to do this anymore. I'm sorry, my friends, it's been fun, enjoy yourselves. Good-bye."

Morgan's fantasy was dashed as my dreams were realized, and I felt bad for a bit, but was then carried away in Stacy's pick-up and all was good. Better than ever. And one week later, we'd spent five nights together and in her arms all darkness was vanquished, all became light.

The morning sun was of a different hue, the evening sunset now only beautiful by her side. Her soft shoulders, the way she kissed, the endless infinite look in her brown eyes, the way her hand felt in mine, the way she leaned into me when we walked to the store.

How I fell. How happily I fell for her. How I sank into her arms, how I lost myself in her kiss, how her scent intoxicates me at night, how we talk in bed until the faint light of dawn sneaks through the drawn curtains, how she reads the Sunday paper on my bed at Cedar Manor (she's sipping coffee wearing only a T-shirt), how sad she almost looks whenever we have to part, how we talk on the phone all the time, how I miss her if she's not here, how fast it all happened, how right it all seems, how good it somehow turned out.

Epilogue

The train out of Mexicali stops at Benjamin Hill to hook up with the train out of Nogales. It was late afternoon, and the Sonoran Desert still roared with heat. Stacy and I got out to stretch our legs and eat the last chicken sandwiches and cookies my Mom had packed for us in San Diego.

I'd pawned the gun and with the cash I'd made from Morgan, decided to take a trip. Stacy couldn't wait to go, and all was hot and sweet and good and the Love stood strong in its eager first steps. We drove her pick-up down the coast, Big Sur and San Simeon, Santa Barbara and then San Diego.

Ole Sis was now a mom. A baby boy cooed and spit in her arms. He was as tiny and sweet as could be. The Baby. A Son of a Mailman, just like myself. I promised to watch out for him.

And Cedar Manor? Cedar Manor was no more. It could never be anymore. Mrs. Park was gone forever.

Carp I was glad to be rid of. I bought Billy a lava lamp, a real nice one. He seemed quite pleased.

And Brady? I don't know. Nothing ever seemed to affect him. When I left, he was still at Cottage D. Still workin' at the Shack. Drinkin' beer, hangin' with his girl. I figure he'll still be there when I get back. I'll look him up when I do. Maybe we'll get a beer or go see Billy and I'll tell them how Mexico was. Whether Love can last.